About the Author

Jaroslavas Melnikas is a Lithuanian of Ukrainian descent. He studied at Lvov University and at the M. Gorki Institute of Literature in Moscow. He has written six books of fiction and a collection of philosophical essays in Lithuanian, as well as several books of poetry and prose in Ukrainian and a novel in French. He is the winner of the BBC Book of the Year for the stories in this collection.

About the Translator

Marija Marcinkute studied English Language at Vilnius University. She set up an English language school in Vilnius shortly after the fall of the Communist regime. She translated business books from English into Lithuanian and has worked as an interpreter in Lithuania, England and America. In 1996 she moved to Spain, where she lived for two years working as a translator and teacher before moving to England in 1998. In England she gained a master's degree in Applied Linguistics. She works as a translator and interpreter.

Jaroslavas Melnikas

The Last Day

Translated from Lithuanian
by Marija Marcinkute

Noir

First published in Lithuanian as Rojalio kambarys

Published by Noir Press Ltd.
www.noirpress.co.uk
noirpress@hotmail.com

Cover design by Le Dinh Han
Cover photo by Jake Hills (Unsplash.com)
Proofreading and editorial: Susan Last, Sheelagh Gallagher, Joy Collishaw
Noir Press is deeply grateful for the generous support of Arts Council England and the Lithuanian Culture Institute in bringing this book to publication.

Supported using public funding by
ARTS COUNCIL
ENGLAND

978-0995560048

Printed and bound in Great Britain by Clays Ltd, Elcograf S.p.A.

Contents

The Last Day

(1)

At first it just seemed bizarre. Three hundred thousand people from all over the world filed a lawsuit against the madman in whose warehouse the eight million volumes were heaped. He had poured nearly all his wealth into printing the thick volumes. It was blasphemy. He was obviously mad. Only a lunatic would print the dates of the deaths of everybody on the planet. Then, as if that wasn't enough, having pulled that fast one, he immediately lost the ability to speak. Whether he had truly been deprived of speech nobody knew, but he never uttered a word from the moment the police arrested him. In fact, he didn't react in any way to their questioning. Then, soon after, he died during a routine interview. His death was odd. He fell from his chair, as if he had been shot by an arrow. The investigator's assistant, who witnessed the incident, said it had been exactly like that, as if an arrow let fly by some Indian had flown through the window and pierced the heart of the offender. There was, of course, no arrow and the windows had not only been closed, but were also tightly covered by a metal shutter throughout the investigation.

In fact, the whole story seemed very odd at first sight. You could understand it, perhaps, if somebody were to lose all their money to gambling, or just gave it away to a loved one. Or even to a beggar in the street. That kind of thing you could explain, one way or another. Any kind of madness can be explained. But to gather information on everybody living on the planet and to print the date of their death, that's hard to get your head around. It was too much. And that was what caused the horror.

At first, the newspapers treated it as if it was a joke, or black humour, but they soon turned angry and critical. Who wants to know the date of their death? The phones glowed red as millions of housewives called in to the offices of newspapers, the TV channels and the police. It was reported that the maniac had been arrested after the wife of the president discovered she would die in four years and five days, while the president had been promised a long life.

Other details leaked out too. The prisoner, it seemed, had been able to gain access to the international databases, so it was quite easy for him to get hold of the names and surnames of everybody on the planet. The rest was simply a question of time and technology.

The whole thing might have been just another one of those sensational incidents that nobody remembers after a month or so, if it had not been for the newspapers. Having quietened down for a while, the headlines blazed again. Reports were coming in from relatives of the recently deceased; people were dying exactly as the *Book of Fates* had predicted. It was incredible, but true. It soon became clear that there were no recorded exceptions. Even those who, knowing the date of their death, had spent the day at home, still died from some cause. Most often they would have a heart attack, but sometimes kidneys or other organs failed. Many started to feel ill long before the fateful date and then, on the assigned day, the illness would reach its climax. Those who deliberately avoided showing any interest in the *Book of Fates* or simply hadn't heard about it (there were such people), often died in street accidents or killed themselves in the bath, struck by some psychological crisis. People were also murdered in accordance with what the book said. The killers were not aware, of course, that they were killing on the *right* day.

In short, it was terrifying. Somebody set fire to the warehouse where the books were stored, and they were reduced to ashes. It had been too much, psychologically, for some people to bear. But, it turned out, there were other warehouses with more copies of the books. In addition to that, the dates had been stored on discs; you simply had to insert the disc into your computer, and type in your name or the name of a relative . . .

How was it possible? It soon became clear that some kind of higher power did indeed exist. Nobody tried to deny it any longer. Opinion was divided only on whether it was God, or some kind of technological Higher Intelligence. If it was God, then why had He chosen to reveal himself through the random writer of the *Book of Fates*? Why He had chosen such a means and what it all meant was incomprehensible. Perhaps aliens controlled fate, or even programmed it. Maybe they simply handed over the data digitally to the person who worked at the electronic centre – a computer download, as it were. But again, why? For what purpose?

Despite all this, life went on. It may seem odd, but it didn't stop. As an experiment some lunatic killed himself before the 'appointed' time. Then several thousand others lost their nerve too. It turned out it was possible to die before your time, which seemed illogical and many found it difficult to understand. However, living longer wasn't possible. Nobody was able to do that.

So, most people just carried on with their lives. What else could they do? Though people knew the exact date they were going to die, the fact didn't put any bread on the table. They had to go out and earn it. For themselves and their children. The children knew nothing. They were the only ones who were able to carry on living like everybody else had done before. The happy ones!

(2)

My wife was already asleep when I got home from my friend's. At that time there were not many discs available. Each disc contained only the names starting with a particular letter. It wasn't easy for somebody wanting the information to access it. Lena had told me that she did not wish to know; she was worried that she would not be able to carry on living. Most people reacted in that way. In many countries governments had issued decrees ordering the confiscation and destruction of the books and discs. But if somebody really wanted to know, there was always a means of getting the information, even in those countries.

'Kolya, whatever for?' My wife asked, when she learned about my need to know the truth. 'Please, don't go.'

'But, Lena . . . This is the truth.'

'Why do we need it, Kolya?' Tears rolled down her cheeks. 'Yes, it's true, we're all going to die. Just let it be. Our Sonia, our little Igor, you, me, we are all going to die. But now we are living. Now we need to live.'

I swore to her that I wouldn't try to find out the date, but then I went to Periturin's and found out everything. We sat at his computer and Periturin gulped as he spoke.

'Look, Kolya, you're going to die on the sixth of May, and I'll die a year later, on the fourteenth of April.'

The silly smile didn't slip from his face. As though he didn't understand.

'And your Lena . . .'

'Shut up, you bastard!'

I hit Periturin in the face and he began to weep. Afterwards it stuck me that Periturin was going to die, and I had hit him on the jaw for no reason. And I wept too.

When I got home, my head was clearer than it had ever been before. Lena was sleeping, breathing barely noticeable, dressed in a light blue nightie. The lids of her eyes trembled as if she were seeing something terrible in her dreams.

Lena would die in twelve years, and I in sixteen. What would we do during our remaining years? Those few, pitifully few, years. But we had more than poor Klava, Periturin's wife; she had only two years left. I sat on the edge of my wife's bed in the half-light and wondered. I was surprised, though, at the direction my thoughts took; there was something terrible in those thoughts. In my feelings too. Because, though I was sad that I would live longer than Lena and go on to live a further four years on my own, I was still happy, somehow, that we were luckier than Periturin and his wife.

Both their children would die young, like our Igor, who would die at fourteen. Our Sonia would live to be eighty-four!

I stood up and went to the children's bedroom. Sonia slept like a little angel, half uncovered, breathing through her nose. She barely fitted in her tiny bed. Soon we would have to buy a bigger one for her. I smiled and went to bed.

I didn't look at Igor . . .

(3)

I don't know why, but from that day, from that evening, to be exact, I have loved Sonia more than Igor. Though it should have been the other way around. Sonia had been granted a long life; it would probably be her fate to become a mother, to prolong the tribe, and I badly needed to pour all of myself, as much as I could, into her. Igor, on the other hand, would die when he was fourteen. So very young. It would be cruel, of course, knowing the truth, not to invest in him. But what for? I had no answer to that.

'Dad, when I grow up, will I be a pilot?'

'Yes, Igor, of course.'

What would he be able to achieve in life? Would he experience falling in love? What would he learn?

We were out of money, so I went to the job centre to find some work. They offered me a position in a company that paid a pittance. Nobody pays good money when you start. If you work hard, in time you may get a normal wage. That was the absurdity of the situation! Knowing that I would die in fifteen years and that I would have to work for a pittance. To labour for a slice of bread? Exactly. That was your fate.

And so I went to work for my 'slice of bread'. Those at the top of the company were raking in the money, and it was I who made that money for them, which was what made it so painful. They were the owners and I was their petty clerk, and it was not them but I who was begging to be given the position.

Lena would get so tired that when she got home from work, she would fall onto the bed and lie there for half an hour. The less you get, the more you sweat. Why waste your life? But what else can you do? A bit of money requires a big effort, a lot of money requires . . . well, it requires a big effort too, but of a different type. But can you compare yourself to those bosses?

Unexpectedly, my mother and father arrived. My mother would die in a year, my father in three years' time. We were talking about cabbages when my father stood up and said, 'I told you your profession was no use, but you didn't listen to me.' Why was he so worked up? He only had three years left. My mother complained about her heart problems.

Sonia, who would live to the age of eighty-four and witness the end of the century, was learning to walk, holding onto her grandmother's finger.

On Thursday, Periturin called and invited me to go fishing. It cheered me up and I decided to take the day off. I knew they would be annoyed, but I couldn't not go.

The fishing was wonderful. Periturin caught eight crucian carp, and I three tench and four crucian carp.

'This is the life, Kolya!' Periturin said.

'And it feels like the *Book of Fates* doesn't exist at all!'

'Yes.'

Birds sang in the bushes, and the breeze blew small waves across the water towards us.

'Beautiful,' Periturin said.

'Yes.'

'Perhaps it's all just nonsense,' Periturin said.

'What?'

'Well, the book. I think it's nonsense.'

'You're talking rubbish.' I lifted my head and looked at him. 'There's not been a single exception.'

'So far.' Periturin changed the bait on his line. 'That's the way it will be until Friday and on Saturday it will stop.'

'How so?'

'What, do you think it can't happen? How do you know?'

He swung his arm and cast the line as far as he could. From that day, I started to see things in a slightly different way. It was true, why couldn't such a thing be possible? At first nobody had even imagined that you could die before your allotted date, but it turned out you could. And anyway, so far there was no definitive data available. All known deaths corresponded to the predicted dates, but was it possible to check everyone who was supposed to have died that day? It would have been very difficult. So then, why was everybody so convinced that there were no exceptions? Perhaps, somewhere in the jungles of Africa, somebody who should have died the day before might still be living the day after. And if there was one exception, then there could be another, and a third and so on.

* * *

Later, lots of people were amused by the confusion. People whose names, surnames and parents' names were the same couldn't work out which death date was theirs. If the *Book of Fates* had been created by God, how come He had allowed such misunderstandings to arise? If he wanted people to know the day of their death, why hadn't He thought about the people whose names were identical? And if it was that deranged millionaire who had allowed the confusion to creep in, why hadn't God corrected him?

There were other misunderstandings. What time zone were the dates in? You had to work that out yourself, calculating the time according to where the millionaire lived. The *Book of Fates* itself didn't have a single word to say about it.

And, finally, what about those who were only now being born? They were not included in the books. If a new prophet didn't turn up, the next generation would live normal lives, as we all had lived when the book did not exist. Was it an experiment? But why?

(4)

A very strange situation unfolded in the country and across the whole planet. Everybody was convinced that a divinity existed. But where was it? The sun shone, as always, the sky was still there, as were the clouds, the trees and animals. The world hadn't changed; everything was alive, vibrant, but the hidden divinity was nowhere to be found. There was just that book, which had appeared out of nowhere. That simply infuriated everybody. God, if you decide to reveal that you exist, and in such an original manner, then show yourself! In what shape? Well, you know best. We'll wait for you in the square and you can show up, the height of a five-storey building at least, so it's clear right away that you're God. Or in the sky, so we can see your face among the clouds. And then we can talk. Who you are, who we are, what death is and what it's all for. We really want to know; who needs this ridiculous fear? If we don't know anything, we're left trembling like rabbits. Why do you hide from us what you know? Just say, 'It's this and that, you've been created for this and that, you live, you are this and that.' Tell us, 'Don't be afraid of death because it's not death at all. I am here and you are here. And you are all mine.'

No, this all is nonsense. There is no need. If such a conversation happened, how would we live afterwards? How would we hammer a nail? How would we grub for pennies in factories? It's not possible to survive seeing God and talking straight with him. We would freeze in horror and wouldn't be able to carry on living. But you need to live; so long as you don't know the real meaning of things, then life goes on. The meaning of life is not to know the meaning. If you found it out, there would be no meaning to life any more.

Irrespective of the situation, life went on. Newspapers, the TV and radio threw themselves into the new topic; we had to get our heads around the state of affairs. After the *Book of Fates*, the world couldn't be the same as it had been before: it was a world in which almost everyone knew or could find out when they would die! Soon, to my amazement, I discovered there were stormy discussion panels, talk shows, and even comedy programmes on the new topic. And, what's more, the new topic was discussed in a relaxed manner, as people sipped wine, along with life's trivia and amusements. A girl whose death the *Book of Fates* had predicted for the following day, was broadcast to millions of viewers on live TV; she mumbled something about 'goodness', 'peace' and 'universal love'. It was enough to send you crazy. Two famous comedians joked with each other (and the whole nation):

'Are you free tomorrow?'

'Tomorrow? Hmm . . . Tomorrow I can't. I have to die.'

(Laughter off screen.)

One morning I told Lena about her death; I couldn't hide it any more.

'I know when I'm going to lose you,' I said as I shaved.

'So, you found it out anyway?' she asked, a little angrily. 'So, when then?'

'In twelve years' time.'

'So soon?' Lena said. She was scrubbing a pot in the kitchen. 'I thought I might have longer.'

'And I'll die in sixteen years' time!' I shouted to make sure that she could hear me from the kitchen.

Earlier, she had said that she wouldn't be able to live knowing her date of death. So what would happen now?

I finished shaving and was about to leave. Lena was fussing with the pot.

'Get some bread while you're out, if you can,' she said without taking her eyes off the pot. 'There's not a single slice left.'

I looked at her, bewildered.

'And call Maria Fedorovna about Sonia.' Our daughter had been struggling with her maths homework.

I stood in the doorway waiting to hear what else she would say. But she continued, working with rapid movements, dropping something into the boiling water in the pot.

'Are you still here?' she asked, noticing that I still stood hesitating in the doorway.

'Lena,' I said. 'I just told you such an important piece of news and you . . .'

'What?' she moved away from the pot, suddenly, an onion in her hand, and fixed her eyes on me. 'So what? What does it change?'

'What do you mean "what"?'

'So what? Is there no need to eat then? Probably you will want to eat? At lunch time?'

'But . . .' I didn't know what to say.

'Or maybe it's okay for Sonia to fail her mathematics?'

'But we will . . .'

'What's the difference? Why do we need to think about it now? How does it help?'

I couldn't believe my ears. I turned around in silence and left. Yes. I had had a limited understanding of my wife.

(5)

The most interesting thing was that we never spoke about the topic again, and nothing changed, nothing at all; we even had quarrels about trifles, like before. Only, occasionally, I would remember that if we trusted that damned *Book of Fates*, time was ticking . . . It was a nightmare; you knew the hour of your death exactly and couldn't do anything about it.

And then, one after another, books started coming out: *The Wisdom of Final Knowing*, *The Meaning of the Sign from Above*,

The Theory and Practice of Leaving. Our philosophers and psychologists rushed to bring something out on the topic while it was hot; knowing their own death date, they still pumped it for money. Of course, people rushed to buy the books and read about it all. A million copies! And I, too, couldn't stop myself from buying them. In their opinion life was better now than ever before. 'Death is no longer a nasty surprise'; 'A person now can look it straight in the eye and calculate his energy'. Companies organizing 'leaving parties' were emerging. As anybody could find out their death date, many began to turn it into an event, like a wedding, or a christening.

One Sunday, Periturin called me inviting me to his acquaintance's 'leaving party' (as they were calling them). To be more exact it was Periturin's wife's friend's husband. He was the big boss of some company, a vice-president, a rich guy, so to celebrate his 'Leaving Day' (that's what was written on the invitations), he had organized a real feast for some five hundred people. Periturin's wife had, of course, refused to go, so he offered the invitation to me. I went as I had only read about these kind of events, which had become more and more popular in and out of town.

Tables were set outside, under the stars (it was summer), and were loaded with food. A brass orchestra played, people danced. Occasionally, here and there, a firework exploded.

'They're having fun, aren't they?' I said to Periturin when the waiter took us over to one of the tables.

'No, they're crying.'

'No, I'm serious.'

'Well, do you think he's stupid or what? Why would he want mourning on his last day?'

'And where is he?'

'Wait, he'll turn up soon.'

As morning approached, the company (if you can call two hundred people a company) became relaxed and conversation flowed freely; people said whatever came into their heads and it all sounded wise. Profound. Suddenly the tower clock began to strike four. The stairs to the castle lit up and the last chime rang out, together with the sound of a fanfare. Everyone froze. The door opened wide and our host appeared wearing a red jacket and tie, smiling. He descended the stairs, his gait still youthful, and his relatives encircled him at the bottom.

Then, after he had sat down at the table, in the most conspicuous seat, the party resumed.

Four in the morning was midnight in the place where the publisher of the *Book of Fates* had lived. The owner's Death Day had dawned, and he wasn't going to take any risks. He appeared on time, not a second late, in order to die in everybody's presence. It was only then that I understood the meaning of 'death in everybody's presence', which had been so praised recently. It was true, there was something in it.

It had grown light, but the owner was still alive: living, eating, laughing and even dancing with young girls.

'Where's the priest?' I asked Periturin, who was half dozing, half drunk.

He lifted his head and looked at me as if seeing me for the first time.

'He isn't invited to this kind of event. What's there for him to do here?'

And his head went down again.

Everyone waited for the culmination, the vice-president's death, which was the reason we had all had gathered there. The only time it had been possible to experience something similar was probably in the Middle Ages, in a crowd waiting for a public execution.

'I want to raise a toast,' I heard, suddenly, from a loud-speaker above my head. 'You will all stay for a little while, but I am leaving. Tomorrow, I will know what is not available for you. So. To my company, Lotos International, long life and prosperity. Nobody has given it an end date yet.'

'Hip hip, hooray!'

I couldn't see who had shouted so loudly. Then followed the sound of corks popping, and champagne began to flow.

At noon, in the sunshine, everybody began to grow tired. The businessman yawned, barely able to stay on his feet. His wife, a large woman with a deep cleavage and bare back, was drunk and laughed inexplicably, with her legs apart, hiccupping.

Some guests began to glance at their watches and secretly slipped away from the table. Others stayed seated, feeling it was not polite to leave before the vice-president's death, which was the reason they had been invited. The world had definitely been turned on its head. I, too, was about to leave (God knows what Lena must have been thinking of me), when a solemn voice suddenly announced through the loudspeaker:

'Gentlemen! He is leaving, gentlemen! Our host is leaving!'

Everybody craned their necks, or even stood up from their seats, so I wasn't able to see much: just a flash of the host in convulsions, his body trembling like a leaf in a chair that had been raised for everybody to see. Five minutes passed.

'Gentlemen, he is no more! Let's drink to him, gentlemen!'

Everyone stood and drank in silence.

'Now then, dessert.'

The rabbits had had similar convulsions when I cut their throat in the country. I grabbed Periturin's hand and dragged him, more-or-less by force, out to the road where our old Zhiguli stood.

'What ridiculousness!'

'So what?' Periturin said. 'And what's the rush? We haven't had dessert yet.'

'Is that how you're supposed to die?'

'What's the difference? People die the way they wish. Do as you want, I'm going to have some dessert.'

'Go on then!'

I sat by the car and waited.

(6)

Lena was changing. As Igor's death approached (I had told her about it, not being able to withhold it any longer), she became more pensive. She hadn't used to be, but now I would find her sitting in the kitchen, a half-peeled potato in her hand, gazing somewhere into the distance. Our windows faced the town park. I have no idea why, but her sadness gave me such joy; it was closer to my heart than her indifference.

Igor knew too. Children are attracted to what is forbidden: at school everybody knew about everybody – how long they had left to live. Somebody would bring in an extract from the *Book of Fates*; you can't block the road to information. Once, I stopped by a sports stadium. Two boys were hitting each other.

'You're a wimp! A little mummy's boy!' one of them shouted, clenching his fists.

'And you're going to kick the bucket in year nine. Ha! I'm going to live till I'm seventy-eight years old, and you will die!'

'You bastard.' The first one grabbed the offender, forcing him on the ground.

'What are you doing there?' I shouted. 'Stop right away!'

Scared, they ran in different directions.

Yes, the world had changed and not for the better.

When Igor reached thirteen, having wished him happy birthday, we lowered our eyes. What could we say? It wasn't even an illness; at least, then, we could have fought it. At least we could have nursed some hope.

'Igor,' I said, swallowing hard. What could I wish my son, who had begun the last year of his life?

'There's no need, Dad,' Igor said. 'I understand it all anyway.'

He was braver than me, and I respected him for that. I could see he was pleased; he valued my respect. Though can you actually speak of being pleased in this context?

Lena was weeping, pressing Sonia closer to herself. Sonia, who would live to be eighty-four.

I don't know why, but I was hoping for a miracle. 'Only a miracle can save us' – the phrase had meant nothing to me before. Periturin's wife was long dead, as was one of his daughters (the other had five years left), but still I hoped. The world had gone mad. The rich paid incredible sums of money for TV channels to broadcast their Leaving Day live, while people watched their TV screens numb as a famous banker or cinema actor left the world. The tabloids, and even some serious newspapers, printed the list of famous people who would die the next day next to the weather forecast. On New Year's Eve, they wrote about which of the world's 'elite' would die the following year. Special institutes prepared data showing how many new jobs would be freed up (doctors, professors, prosecutors) and the fight for them would start while those leaving us were still alive.

Lena and I prepared ourselves psychologically and materially for Igor's Day, as we called it. We decided Igor's 'send-off' would be for the narrow family circle only; Lena, Sonia Igor and me. That's how people behaved, those who didn't follow the fashion to celebrate their leaving day by inviting guests and so on.

The evening before, we washed, put on clean clothes, sat around the table and ate supper in silence. We decided not to sleep that night; we wanted to be with Igor. Igor behaved as he had never before; it seemed as if it was not him but us who were being seen off. He even tried to joke.

As morning approached, Igor was still alive; even his weak kidneys didn't hurt (he had been born with the condition, having inherited it from Lena). The only thing Lena and I wished was for his leaving to be peaceful, without suffering. Just so long as it wasn't suffocation or some 'blood from mouth' thing. My God, we are such lumps of meat in somebody's hands; do what You want with us.

At lunch time, Lena suddenly started to pray in the bathroom, which she had never done before. My nerve faltered too. Perhaps it was true that it was better to drink, as was recommended? But somehow I didn't want to be drunk on such an occasion.

'Why don't we watch *Katerina from Mexico*?'

We all looked at Igor, surprised; he was referring to the soap opera we had been watching for the last six months.

He was right, it was the wisest decision. Though perhaps a little blasphemous.

We sat down, switched on the TV (it was already getting dark) and suddenly felt a peace and joy (yes! yes!), as if nothing was happening. There was no *Book of Fates*. It was as if we had just sat down, the four of us, as always, warming each other with our bodies and smiles. Indeed, we smiled. It seemed nothing could happen; no hurricane could blow through our safe little world and ruin it.

When the programme ended, the anxiety returned immediately, along with the feeling that we couldn't prevent the inevitable. We did not want to believe it though. It was a nightmare.

Night fell. Sonia nodded off on the settee, while the rest of us sat up, our eyes glued to the television screen, not able to comprehend what was happening (Lena and I, anyway – I could feel her). When would it be? When?

Igor's last day was about to end.

(7)

Igor had still not died. There were a few minutes left before four (midnight by the *Book of Fates* publisher's time), and Lena and I, consumed with horror, while at the same time sensing some miracle, fixed our eyes on the hands of the clock on the wall. The last minute began . . .

'Igor . . .' Lena said. 'My son . . .'

She moved towards him as if wishing to protect him from his fate. I bit my lip. Well . . . Well then . . .

When four o'clock struck, all three of us jumped. Something had happened.

'You're alive, Igor?' I couldn't believe my eyes.

We held onto our joy, bottling it up, as if waiting for some confirmation, our minds whirling; perhaps the clock was fast (though the previous night we had checked it for that very reason). There might have been some mistake . . .

Half an hour passed. An hour. It struck five. Igor (alive, smiling) sat in front of us. We did not understand.

(8)

The *Book of Fates* disappeared as it had come. It was reported that the prophecies had stopped being fulfilled three days before (though the world at large had not discovered this, as the information was not available to everybody). In another two months, everybody had begun to calm down, as people were reassured by the fact that people who had been supposed to die during that time were still living.

Lena and I felt as if we had been born anew; as if we had been given a second chance.

'Let's go to the sea! Tomorrow! To hell with everything!'

We would never have gone on a spontaneous holiday before. Oh God, how we wanted to live!

Though, if you thought about it – what had changed? Had we become immortal? I couldn't even be sure, now, that I would live until the date that had been assigned to me. The more so for Sonia with her eighty-four years. So why did we suddenly feel this strange sense of wellbeing? Why?

The Grand Piano Room

(1)

I used to play the grand piano in my grand piano room. I only had to walk to the end of the corridor and open the door. There, on a specially decorated little table, lay a violin that my father would occasionally play. He would play when I wasn't in there, which could be a little difficult (finding a moment when I wasn't playing the piano, that is). If my father had suddenly felt like running his bow across the violin's strings he wouldn't have felt free to do so whenever he wanted. Clearly, it was a bit of an uncomfortable situation, even if it had only been once that he had approached the door and stopped, hearing the music flowing from beneath my fingers. I don't think there's any doubt that my father's desire to play the violin would have been impeded by my presence in the room; he would have been a little bitter (perhaps not just a little) having hurried to the room, wanting to draw the bow across the strings of his violin, right then, immediately.

Perhaps he would have felt then (for the first time?) that there was someone behind the door, filling his space.

Fortunately, such a situation would have been rare; it couldn't have happened more than once because my father hardly played the violin, while I only spent a couple of hours a week on the grand piano. All of this worry was just conjecture and hypothesising, thank God.

Whenever I felt any kind of need, I always knew where I could go. I would play music in the grand piano room. Everything you might have needed was there and not a thing more. There was a music stand in the corner, a shelf of sheet music, and a bust of Beethoven on the grand piano. On the walls were portraits of composers. And another thing was the acoustics (the walls had been specially treated). There was a vase of flowers on the windowsill. I like emptiness. You would never find a hairbrush next to Beethoven, or a fork or some glue. The hairbrush was in a cabinet in the bathroom, the fork was in the dining room. The tube of glue was in the drawer of my desk, next to some pins, paper clips and other stationery items.

In the same way, my painting was focused on my studio: the canvasses, the paint, the thinners, the gypsum models and the picture frames – everything that created my special world. This space had nothing to do with music, or with forks or hairbrushes and paper clips. And so what if I only went down to the studio (which was located in the warm basement) once a week, or even once a month? That wasn't important. The important thing was that everything there had only one purpose, was dedicated to only one need. Everything was waiting for me. In a haze, I would finish a picture I had started some time before, having finally found the right solution. Then I would forget about the studio again for a while. I never thought about whether I was a professional or just an amateur: I simply painted. I needed to. Occasionally.

So my life revolved slowly around these 'rooms'. At my desk I wrote and thought, in the grand piano room I played the piano, in the studio I painted. I had my meals in the dining room, I washed in the bathroom and slept in the bedroom. In the sitting room, next to the fireplace, I watched TV. I relaxed in the snooker room. We don't need to mention the obvious things like the toilet, with its light blue unit, the woodwork room (I used to like turning wood), and the gym (a sprung floor, a gymnastics wall, weights and other sports equipment). Somehow, it never occurred to me to think about how privileged I was to have all this. Was I a count? A duke? A millionaire's son? Who was I? Was I dreaming? No, that was how I lived. That was the air I breathed. That was me; a different 'me' in each of the rooms.

My parents, my wife and my children were exactly the same. My children had their own room, my wife had a dressing room with mirrors and cosmetics. We all lived very nicely.

Even guests didn't disrupt our spiritual harmony. They did nothing to spoil it, to tarnish that cleanliness, that mirror-sharp clarity (oh, how shiny our floors always were!). Our guests had their own rooms (they often stayed overnight). After dinner with our guests, I would calmly go off to one of my rooms (if I had no business in town that day, of course). And then I no longer felt their presence in our house. They never distracted me from myself, they always remained just guests.

(2)

What I am going to tell you happened unexpectedly, and, most importantly, without any explanation. One morning, feeling the pull of the piano (I just needed to run my fingers across the cool, snow-white keys!), I turned to go to the grand piano room only to find that there was no door at the end of the corridor. No door to the grand piano room! I'm one of those people who only believe in reality to an extent: not totally, as it were. Though nobody could say that I wasn't a rational thinker. However, my reaction to the inexplicable becoming reality is not fast and is never hysterical. I look at something like that primarily as a phenomenon; though it's not clear to me what has happened, it must have some inherent meaning. Because, for goodness sake, a whole room in the house can't just disappear like that without a reason.

So as I was looking at that space on the wall I started to think, and it seemed to me that perhaps I should look at it from the opposite angle: what was strange was not the fact that the piano room had disappeared, but that it had ever actually existed. It was difficult though to establish the boundary between reality and appearance: was it not strange that there, on the smooth surface of the wall, there had once been a door? At least, it felt stranger to affirm that the door had existed, rather than say that it had never been there at all.

However, feeling a little unnerved by such an odd and incomprehensible situation, I plucked up the courage (having decided to avoid hysteria) to talk to my family. It's good that I am circumspect!

'What are you talking about, Jura?' my wife said, glancing at me oddly. 'What door are you talking about?'

She even stroked the smooth surface of the wall.

'Never mind,' I replied with a wary smile. 'Perhaps I'm overtired. I'll go and do some work at the easel to distract myself.'

I went down to the studio. My intuition whispered to me uncertainly: if it turned out that there was no piano room any more, could it be the same with the studio? I chased the thought away as I descended the stairs.

The studio was where it had always been. Closing the door, I let out a sigh of relief. But I knew the piano room too well to believe that it had been a fiction. I recalled all the wonderful moments, the hours spent in the silence and emptiness of the room! I remembered its layout, the shelves for sheet music, the little decorated table for my father's violin. I knew with certainty that Beethoven's bust had stood upon the piano. I had no doubt; the piano room was a reality. But if there was no sign left on the wall where the door had been, if my wife had never heard about it, perhaps it was some other reality.

The strangest thing was that I remembered my wife coming into the room occasionally. Perhaps that too had been a different reality. And my wife, Lucy, perhaps she was somebody else then? At least I wasn't silly enough to start blundering in on such a sensitive issue.

Having recovered somewhat, I suddenly noticed my grand piano in the corner of the studio where I had used to keep a pile of canvases; it was the *same* brand, with the *same* scratch on its leg. There could be no doubt it was the *same* piano, the one from the grand piano room. And on it, in the very *same* place, stood the Beethoven bust.

Looking around, I grew slightly annoyed (which was not typical of me); some of my canvases were piled on the table along with the paint. Some others were stood next to the rack, and the rest had slid under the piano as they probably didn't fit in the gap between the piano and the table. Possibly for the first time in my life I knelt down under the piano in search of the sketches for my paintings. My new, neatly-ironed trousers became covered in dust and in a pinky-purple substance. What was sadder was that the two sketches I did find, as I was looking under the table, were irreparably damaged as they had been lying in paint. I didn't look for the third one.

So the first thing I had to do was tidy the studio. The grand piano room that I remembered so well had been wonderful, but that made little difference now. I had to come to terms with reality, even if it was a very different reality. Different but powerful, as it expressed itself through my irritated state. I had to act to ensure that it stopped irritating me.

To begin with I gathered all the canvases into one place, as before. It turned out that my studio was not that big. Of course, it had been bigger when the piano hadn't take up all the space, but now . . . Now a large corner had been taken, and I had to lean the canvasses against the rack, put some on the paint table and squeeze the remaining ones between the wall and the piano. Whoever had piled them that way (I wasn't totally sure that it hadn't been me), had behaved as if there had been no other solutions. A situation with no solution – those were the words that finally came to mind. This whole thing stank of hopelessness. Well, really, where could I put the canvases?

I wanted them to be all together like they used to be. Like before. I was not used to looking for the thing I needed in three different places.

Mulling over this problem, it suddenly occurred to me that I had been in the studio for about half an hour. And what had I done? That had never happened before. I used to come in and go straight to the easel. Everything had been in the right place – the canvases, the paint, the thinners, the brushes. I just had to pick up a brush and pour out onto the canvas that fleeting feeling, that idea that had excited me and drawn me to the studio in the first place.

But now I was surprised to find that I spent my time doing different things, as if I had forgotten the reason I had gone to the studio. That is, I knew why I had gone, I hadn't forgotten, it was just that I . . . couldn't work. Yes, physically. My paint was covered with canvases. I had to put the canvases somewhere. And now I was racking my brain where to put them. I wasn't thinking about the painting, which was strange. 'I'll put the canvases away and start working,' I told myself. I couldn't think of any better place to put the canvasses than the same corner they had been in. The only other option was to put them on top of the piano, as I couldn't stand the idea of them lying on the floor under the piano.

Now that I could stand in front of the easel, I went to get the paint. Something was wrong and I couldn't work out what it was at first. The light was streaming down from the window in the ceiling. I started to mix the colours. No, they were not right. There was no feeling, no mood, no subconscious thought that had brought me here in the first place.

The feelings were not there. Perhaps I was tired after all the work storing the canvasses?

I stood in the middle of the room, not knowing what to do. It was not clear what I should paint. Nothing struggled to get out onto the canvas. Nothing demanded to be expressed. I suddenly realised I was full of another, unfamiliar feeling. It was anger, resentment. Resentment of what? I glanced at the piano and I realised. I hated the piano. Quietly, almost unconsciously. It shouldn't have been in the studio taking up so much space, overcrowding it so badly.

I thumped up the stairs. Fortunately, I didn't meet anybody on the way. The door, the door to the grand piano room – it should exist. The grand piano room should exist. I wouldn't be able to live without it, there was no way I could.

It wasn't there. Fatuously, I moved my hand up and down the wall.

Then I went down to the studio again and tumbled into a chair. How easy it is to lose your peace of mind. I opened the piano fallboard and ran my fingers across the keys. I needed to calm down. I ran my fingers across the keys again. Something had happened to Chopin – it was not Chopin, definitely not him. It did not sound the same, though my fingers moved the same way on the keyboard. Of course! I smiled to myself, in an attempt to stop the new wave of irritation: the piano lid was pressed down by the canvases. If I took them off, they would have to go under the piano; the others could go in the rack and the rest on the paint table. How many of them there were! There was only one solution – to take them off the piano while playing and then to put them back again when I had finished.

That was what I attempted to do. I managed to put them in a small pile by the door (nobody would come in anyway). So, back to Chopin: one passage, then another. I couldn't work out what had happened to the feelings I had experienced in the grand piano room. Maybe the acoustics were different? Or was it the lighting? I couldn't put my finger on the answer. Perhaps the canvasses or the paint were the problem? The fact was, it was quite crowded in there. Or had I got tired dragging the canvasses over to the door?

I slammed the lid shut. Now I couldn't even leave the studio; to do that I would have to move the pile of canvasses back onto the grand piano.

(3)

The next day I decided to talk to my father about the grand piano room.

'The grand piano room?' My father was surprised. 'What are you talking about, Jura? You need to understand, we haven't got the means. There is a limited amount of space in the house, and what about Lora? Look, she might get married soon. She'll have her own family.'

Lora was my eldest daughter. There was no grand piano room. There never had been. Or if there had been, then it had been in some other reality. My father didn't remember it. He remembered neither the grand piano room, nor the fact that he used to play his violin there. He assured me that he played, as he had always played, in his bedroom. In his bedroom!

'But the acoustics are so bad there!'

'Well, what can you do about it, Jura?'

I had no option but to adjust to these inconveniences, though I didn't believe my father or my wife. I found it difficult to let go of the feeling that the grand piano room had existed. But how was I going to live now? I used to hear the phrase, 'I somehow had to go on living' on other people's lips without understanding what it meant. I had to carry on living, and, having wasted a week mulling things over, I invented a mobile ceiling above the grand piano. Yes, a special ceiling where I could store my canvases. During the week when I was making the ceiling (drawing the plans, ordering, fastening), I couldn't recognise myself. I had never had to do anything like that before. I wouldn't say I liked it. In fact, I hated what I was doing. There used to be a grand piano room and now there was not – and I had to take care of the damn ceiling so that I could somehow carry on with my life. It drove me crazy.

However, when the ceiling was up I calmed down a little. At least the canvasses now had their own place. But the studio felt crowded. The grand piano, the ceiling . . . I tried not to look in the direction of the grand piano. I looked at the birds that came to peck at the crumbs (which I put out on the windowsill every morning). The sun, the birds and there you go! I started painting. Something began to pour out onto the canvas; colours, lines. All was well. Life could go on.

After all, I didn't live in the studio. In general, my life hadn't changed: I still worked at my desk in the office, went to the sitting room to watch the television, played snooker in the snooker room. And my wife would still use her dressing room to do her make-up. Just one thing made me break out into a cold sweat: the thought that what had seemed a random occurrence might not be so random at all. The surface of reality upon which I was standing seemed fragile.

Which is why, when the studio disappeared a year later, I was not only not surprised, but felt happy in a way; a certain logic had been confirmed, some vague presentiment of mine. I was obviously on a journey towards something; I had crossed something that I had to cross. The process was unpleasant and unavoidable and I knew it was pointless to resist it. If I had seen real workmen dismantling the studio brick by brick, or blocking it off brick by brick, then I could have done something about it; I could have fought for it. I could have called the police, appealed to the rights of the private property owner and chased the criminals away with a pistol in my hand. But it had not been that way; everything had happened differently. One fine morning you go down to your studio and find a blank wall instead of a door. A wall you're told was built half a century before. What can you do? You have to accept it and try to comprehend the essence of absurdity: that's how it should be. He who has the power to change reality without workmen, bricks or mortar knows what he is doing.

Of course, that's how it was. Or so I thought, shut away in my office in which now, apart from the desk, the bookshelves, the settee and the armchairs there was also an easel, my canvasses, paint, the rack, sheet music and, of course, the grand piano with the bust of Beethoven on it. Well, at the end of the day, it was possible to live like that. I kept repeating that to myself, attempting to rid myself of the feeling that I was being persecuted by fate. To be honest, what I really wanted was to drag whoever had done this out of the wall by the beard and finish him off on the spot for the dirty trick he had played on me. I wasn't sure what to call him – fate, God or the devil? Still, I felt like finishing him off with twenty sharp swords; to stab each one right through his heart.

I had never known I had such a boiling volcano in me. I hadn't experienced feelings like that before. Generally, I was a good person with a positive outlook on life. I hadn't experienced before, as I did now, the pain of hitting my leg on the grand piano on the way over to my office desk. Or what it meant to stick my fingers into white paint while trying to take some sheet music from the drawer (I was short of drawers in my office and there was no space for a new table or cupboard). In addition to that, I hadn't realised it was possible to knock the bust of Beethoven off while attempting to take a book from the shelf (Beethoven now had a glue-scar on his forehead). I hadn't known a lot of things. I was especially affected by one terrible incident: one of my most precious paintbrushes disappeared. I looked for it for four hours. On principle. I swore I would find it. No matter what, I had to find it (before that I had had no idea what it meant to look for things!). And when I was worn out, I finally found it by chance (I sat down at the grand piano to calm myself and by its dull sound I realised that the brush was stuck between the strings). I began to weep, probably for the first time in my life. I used to be so strong all the time; with my grand piano room and the studio I had no idea that space and order might play such an important role in my life. I had assumed that my strength, my self-composure, my seriousness were all intrinsic to me. So I cried as I pulled the paint brush from the grand piano in my overcrowded office. And I was not myself. I could not identify with this broken man. I understood, though, that I was going off the rails. Probably for the first time in my life.

(4)

Meanwhile, my family behaved as if nothing had changed. They would drop in my office, not at all surprised that it was cramped and chaotic (the more I fought against the chaos, the more it enslaved me). As if it had always been like that. And I didn't doubt that was what they thought. I was afraid to even mention the studio to them, to ask them whether it used to exist or not. It was clear, anyway, what they would have said. They thought it was normal, from what I could see, that one room should serve as a grand piano room, an office and a studio. It was this that shook me most. If they had been, say, as exasperated as I was by how cramped it was in there, and said something about the piano room, or about the studio . . . But, the closest they came to this was when they said things like, 'It's true, it is a bit cramped in here; we should replace the grand piano with an upright. That's the solution.' Replace my grand piano with an upright! I felt like I had begun to disappear, bit by bit. I sensed that something undefined was emerging in place of me; a ball of nerves. I was not clear what.

And that was worst of it. How could I paint when in front of my eyes there stood a grand piano, as well as my writing desk? They were different, totally different worlds. Could it be that nobody understood that? Those worlds couldn't and shouldn't be associated with each other.

'You don't know life yet,' my father said to me once.

What did he mean?

I understood a couple of months later. Summer came. I tried to adjust myself to my office situation (I had no real choice but to ignore the surroundings). I had to reconstruct myself psychologically. *I had to* – it was easy to say, but that readjustment left me dry! There was no *me* left. It was unbearable to see how, having lived like a lord, all my essence was now focused on this struggle with myself, this fight with circumstances! Silently, I cursed my fate, my situation. I couldn't imagine it being worse.

Unfortunately, not long after, I discovered it could be.

One evening, after dinner, in the most disgusting mood, I headed towards my office and . . . it was not there. I couldn't find it at all. To be honest, I should have expected it. It was the logical next step. But for some reason I had been unable to imagine such a thing. I could understand that my space was getting more constricted, but that it should disappear altogether? Totally? How was that possible? This time I didn't touch the wall with my hands, I kicked it. I knew it was absurd. And I kept kicking it – because it was absurd.

'What is it, Jura?' My wife came out into the corridor. 'What's the noise about?'

'The neighbours.' I said, squashing the hurricane of feelings with an enormous exertion of willpower.

'They're constantly doing repairs,' my wife mumbled unhappily.

And then I realised what I had said. What neighbours? We lived in a detached house! Freezing, horrified, I recalled my wife's reaction: she had not been surprised by my explanation!

That meant that there, behind the wall, there really were some neighbours? I didn't want anybody living behind my wall. The idea that other people were living behind the wall would interfere with my breathing. Biofields exist. Other people's biofields would affect my brain – it was common knowledge.

I threw myself towards my office to shut myself away – to calm down – to think it all through! I moved, then stopped. I was no longer able to find refuge in my own little office, no matter now cramped it had been. All that was left was to kick the hard wall – at the space where the door used to be.

But where, then, was my space? I rushed to the snooker room: there was no snooker room either. There was our living room with a TV and armchairs. There was no fireplace. And there stood my desk and my books on the bookshelves. Bookshelves! Would I have to work in there, then? I turned around and went to the bedroom. I found my canvasses heaped up in there, and my paint, and next to them, against the wall, my piano. Not my grand piano!

From now on I would have to work at my desk with the television on in the background, or my wife, my children and my parents would have to do without the living room and the television. But that was impossible. Just as impossible as me trying to find refuge in there. It would be better in the bedroom. But . . . No, there was no space for a desk in the bedroom. There was a bed, the piano and my canvasses.

I slumped into a chair. This couldn't be true. I had kept silent and suffered, but a line had been crossed. That was it. Enough.

I stood up and went to the kitchen where my wife was.

'I can't do this,' I said to her. 'I need an office.'

'What do you mean?' She stopped washing the dishes. 'Is it that bad in the living room?'

'Lucy, everybody watches television in the living room.'

'But you're used to it,' my wife said. 'You never complained before.'

I couldn't recall ever working in a room full of people, and particularly when they were watching television. But if my wife said so, could it have been possible? God forbid! But it was possible. I would have to adjust to it. I would have to turn into the person she was talking about, but only because I had no other options. It was possible that in some other reality (which my wife had in mind) I used to work in the living room. But why? How could I?

'You know that there is no other space for it.'

She said it as if it were obvious. She accepted the reality of the situation in the same way that it would be accepted by any soberly-thinking person. Just whose reality?

I headed towards the bedroom. There was no need to inspect the woodwork room: if it had still been there, I would have set up my office in it. Anywhere at all, just not in the living room.

I inspected every corner of the bedroom in an attempt to understand the situation I had found myself in. It wasn't long before I came across my turning bench: it was in the wardrobe, behind the coats! This proved that in this reality I was still myself, with all my needs. I was still the same me, just a lamentable version. What had changed was that now I had a windowsill in the bedroom to fasten my lathe to instead of my woodwork room. The paint on it was peeling. Was it worth living?

(5)

Meanwhile, the others went on with their lives without asking any questions. And that was fully understandable. Nobody, apart from me, seemed to know anything about the grand piano room, the studio or the woodwork room and the snooker room. They lived in that one possible reality, while I knew there was another.

I soon realised that in the living room there was not only the television and my desk, but also a sofa bed on which my parents slept at night. Their bedroom had somehow disappeared. They had put so much effort into supporting me that they had never had one of their own. This I could never believe. I clearly remembered my father and mother going to their own bedroom. My father had had his own office! Something had tampered with reality, something had moved, broken down.

What in fact saved me, was a certain mistrust with which I gazed at the reality around me. I felt, I understood and I saw that there was a different life. And I was very well informed about it. If I wasn't breathing it, how then would I have such specific knowledge about it, such clear feelings?

My surroundings, as far as I could make out, seemed to be changing faster and faster: because of this I was almost certain that it was not an 'eternal wheel', but rather a one-way process with its own logic, which was rushing towards its destination. Only I did not know where that destination was. Once, when I discovered we didn't have a separate dining room any more (we had meals in the kitchen, by the cooker), and later, when I realised there was no nursery (for some time, unknown to me, our children had been sleeping in our bedroom!), I grew calmer somehow. It was so absurd, so incredible, that it almost stopped hurting. I lay on the bed and watched how, there, in the same bedroom, my wife bathed our fully naked children (the bathroom seemed to have disappeared as well), and I smiled. Was it possible to believe it all? The splashes of water and soap on the floor, my canvasses leaning against the wall, stood in the soapy water. And in the wardrobe – my turning bench. In the wardrobe!

'Are you okay, Jura?'

'Why?'

'Your smile seems a bit strange. Have you bought a candle?'

'What for?'

'I told you already. You'll have to smear the zip. Lora's shoe won't zip up.'

I kept on smiling.

'And sew her school bag.'

She went into the same wardrobe and pulled out an awl and a thick thread.

'There!'

She threw the bag towards me.

I took the awl, turned it in my hand, then sat down and began to sew my daughter's ripped bag. I could hear how, on the other side of the wall, in the living room, my mother was quarrelling with my father about something (a couple of days before I had discovered my father's violin on the cupboard in the hall, all covered with dust).

(6)

There was no question of doing any painting. In order to take the easel out of the wardrobe, first I would have to pull out the turning bench. Then I would have to find the paint, which was in the corner behind the hats. The only chair in the room would have to be put onto the bed, otherwise there would be no space for the easel. The worst thing was that I couldn't step back to see the canvas from a distance. There was no stepping back at all. Right behind me stood the bunkbed. Lora was nearly an adult – a woman – and she slept in a child's bed above her younger brother. Was that normal? And was it normal that children should sleep in the same bedroom as us? And was it possible?

Once, trying to reach my paintbrush, I knocked over the night pot under the bed. Was it normal that my wife and daughter had turned our bedroom into a toilet?

'But, Jura,' my wife said, surprised, 'do you really want Lora to run to the closet outside when it's so cold? You know how that all ends.'

There was one thing I couldn't understand, how could they all bear it? Where did they get such patience from?

'What happened to our toilet?' I asked, not able to hold myself back. 'We had a toilet, we had a bathroom.'

My wife looked at me as if I had been struck by lightning.

'What are you on about, Jura?'

I left the room. I knew that she would say something like, 'We've always gone to the closet outside. What's up, Jura?' It was impossible to prove that until quite recently (as it seemed to me) I had seen my wife and daughter use the bathroom and toilet. That was the thing; I didn't doubt my wife's sincerity for a second. Or the fact that she didn't remember a thing. But it had been like that, I was certain. Like with the grand piano room.

A couple of months later, I was unsurprised to see my parents carrying their night pots down the hall. And, though I knew that they didn't have any choice, still they were in some ways diminished in my eyes. It was hard to explain. My father used to wear brand-new clothes (I remembered his beautiful fingers, the violin on his shoulder). Could that be him groaning in the living room (they had no bedroom of their own)? And I could hear all this. What respect could I have after that? Pity or understanding – yes. But it is enough to pity a person once, or see them powerless, and they lose something for ever. Something which I had so valued in our relationship. And all that sneaking around (running out with a night pot so nobody could see), and that suspiciously cheap smell of perfume in the living room after 'it' . . .

'I can see how all this is annoying you.' My wife was able to guess my mood. 'Just wait a bit, spring is around the corner, and then summer. It will be better.'

She was comforting me! I took out my old paintings and looked at them: God, how much freedom! The flight! What inspiration! And they were trying to tell me that I had never had my own studio?

I had stopped painting a long time before; even to try to paint would prove meaningless. After I had found everything and set it out, there would be nothing to express anymore. And my children would keep coming in every now and then to get something. They would listen to their cassette player (it was their room too, wasn't it?).

The kitchen had shrunk as well. I deduced this from the fact that for some time we had been eating in turns, rather than all together. My parents ate first, then the children, and finally my wife and I. My wife, children and parents assured me that this had always been the case. But it wasn't even a kitchen, for God's sake, it was more like a pantry and a store room together. There were some bowls and a child's bath above our heads. On the kitchen table, which was small anyway, was a sewing machine tray with the machine itself on top of it, and on top of that, an iron and some dirty forks.

'You are unhappy again, Jura.' My wife, though she sometimes sensed my mood, could not really understand it. 'Where would you suggest I put all this instead?'

What could I say to her? Where is my piano? I couldn't even run my fingers over the keys to remember it; it seemed (so my wife asserted) that I had sold it. When our children grew older, we had needed a bunkbed for them. So I was even capable of that? Even if through force of circumstance?

(7)

Life went on. And this, I realised, was my reality. There wouldn't be another. And I wasted it left, right and centre, every day. I didn't paint (where would I?), I didn't play (on what would I play?), I didn't write (my desk went to my children, they used it in turns). And what I felt and experienced wasn't even worth talking about. My daily life was spent dealing with domestic issues. I struggled to extend the top bunk for Lora's legs (for the past year, she hadn't been able to stretch her legs), I mended the iron which broke once a week.

'We should get a new one.'

'On what money, Jura?'

We had no money, it seemed. Somehow, it had never struck me before.

The only thing that saved me was the feeling that somebody was in some way experimenting on me. I was in awe of myself; how come I didn't explode? Didn't break everything in reach? All that marasmus I mean, not life itself. My wife valued my relative patience even if she couldn't understand where it came from. Somehow, nothing seemed serious. It was, of course. Was it serious to warm up pots of water and then find somewhere in the flat to have a wash? Or to play cards, the six of us, in the living room in the evenings? I was just about to deal an ace and a king when I shivered; what was I doing there? Who was this playing cards? It seemed reminiscent of a scene from a horror movie. Another time I caught myself, with my wife and my father, all quite tipsy, giggling and gossiping about the neighbour's wife who was cheating on her husband with her boss. I stood up right away, went into the kitchen and put my head under cold water.

'Where are you, Jura?' I heard my wife's voice from the living room, sounding drunk and content. My Lucy never used to drink alcohol. I appeared in the doorway, my face wet, water running down it. In the smoke-filled room, face on the table, my inebriated father was muttering something. Next to him sat an unfamiliar old woman with a silly smile on her face.

'What's up, hic?' My wife hiccupped loudly. 'Here, have another drink.'

'Lucy,' I said. 'When did you start drinking?'

'Oh, I can't anymore!' She burst into laughter, her massive breasts shaking. 'What a joker you are, Jurcik. Sit here.'

I turned around and went to our bedroom (in the kitchen my daughter was with some unfamiliar guy). Quickly, I tried to work out what was happening. But I had no chance. In the bedroom, a dirty man was sleeping on my bed with his shoes on.

'Get out of here,' I said trying to tame my temper. 'Quick!'

'You what, Feofanov?' he said, surprised. 'Oh, I get it.' He looked me up and down attentively.

'I'm totally sober!' I said. 'And I insist, I insist . . . Out! Get lost! Now!'

The man's face changed immediately. He sat up in bed.

'You get lost yourself,' he said angrily. 'You didn't even knock on the door.'

I ran from the room.

'Lucy!' I said breathlessly to my merry wife. 'There's . . . There's . . .'

'What is it?' she asked, seeming somehow devious.

'There's a man in our bedroom.'

'Oh, it's Konkin, our neighbour.' She stood up with difficulty and tottered across to me. 'My dearest, you are totally . . .'

She leant against me and began to weep.

It was, I realised, all just a dream and I laughed to myself. So, another family lived in our bedroom. That is, they had moved in. With whose permission? When?

'My darling,' my wife said, 'they've been living here with us all their lives. Have you forgotten everything?'

'Who are they?'

'Konkin with his wife and children.'

'Where are his children?'

'They'll be back in the evening.'

'Where do we live? Where do we sleep? Where do we eat? Where do our parents sleep? Our children?'

'Here.' My wife was surprised and waved her hand to indicate the room. 'Here's our sofa bed, and behind the screen, your parents' bed.'

'And Lora?'

'Lora and Liosha sleep behind the wardrobe, where else?'

I went to the wardrobe; it was true, behind it a mattress lay on the floor, and above it a crib swayed.

'Be quiet, Verochka is sleeping,' she whispered.

'Verochka?'

'Yes, our granddaughter.'

'Where do we eat?'

'In the kitchen.'

'And where do the Konkins eat?'

'We have a shared kitchen, Jura.'

My wife, though drunk, honestly pitied me.

I ran out into the corridor; right there had been the door to the grand piano room, and then further down the corridor had been my office and at the end were the stairs to the studio. And on this side, further along, there had been a snooker room and my father's office.

'Lucy.' My wife was in exactly the same place I had left her, in the doorway, with a silly smile on her face. 'Where are my paintings?'

'What paintings?'

'The ones I used to paint, in oil?'

'So, you're a painter?' My wife let out a nervous laugh.

'I used to paint, you should remember.'

'When? A hundred years ago?'

'It's not important. Where are they?'

'They could be in the kitchen, on the cupboard.'

I went in to the kitchen. My daughter, in her nightie, was quarrelling with the same man.

I forced myself past them without a word. There were, indeed, some rolled-up, dusty, cobwebbed canvasses. I cleaned off the cobwebs and had a look; nothing had changed. They were still the same: new, bright and free. The paintings had been made in the studio, in the large empty hall fragrant with sun and paint. It was only there that they could have been painted. It was the best proof I had that I wasn't going mad; nobody could explain how I could have painted them if I had spent my entire life here, sharing a room with my parents, my wife and children. God himself had given me this sign so that I didn't fall into despair. He had saved the evidence, so that I wouldn't believe in the life I was living at that moment.

'Dad, why are you whimpering here?' I suddenly heard my daughter's voice. 'It's bad enough as it is. You need to do something about your nerves, I noticed a long time ago.'

'Jurij Vladimirovich,' the man with a beard interrupted, 'I know a psycho-neurologist personally. I do, I swear.'

Without a word I went back out into the corridor. In the living room my wife and my father, who seemed half asleep, were waiting for me. So the Konkins lived in our bedroom. I stopped midway down the corridor: that meant I had nowhere to go.

(8)

The worst thing was that I had become the very essence of irritability. From morning till night, I suffered constantly from this irritation. The sobering thought that everything that was happening to me was not true, not serious, lasted but for a moment; it would disappear suddenly, giving way to prickliness and anger. For longer stretches of time, I did not feel like myself; something held me firmly in its grip. It wouldn't allow me to come to my senses. Their problems, thoughts and gossip overwhelmed me, everywhere – in the kitchen, the corridor, in the living room. Or, what was worse, they would thrust an awl into my hand or a chisel, or a hammer and I was constantly required to fix something, make something, renew something. Endlessly. 'Look, the leg of this small chair is totally loose.' And I would fix the leg. I helped everybody pleasantly enough, and they all realised it and valued it. But, God, that was what my life consisted of!

One night, getting into bed, I discovered somebody else's body instead of my wife's. I shouted so loudly that a commotion broke out.

'Why are you yelling?' my wife asked. She was, apparently, on the other side of me.

'And who is this?' I asked, the fright having caused me to lose my head.

'What the hell?' the unfamiliar body said. 'I have to start work early tomorrow.'

'That's Konkin,' my wife said. 'Go to sleep.'

'What, Konkin?' I sat up.

'You know, the Konkins live with us,' my wife explained.

'Why?'

'Where else could they live then? On the street?'

I ran out into the corridor in my underwear. There was no door to the bedroom. I turned to go to the kitchen, to shut myself away until I could get my head around the situation. If I was able to live in the same room with my children and my parents, then I could manage with total strangers as well. Oh, I didn't fully know myself yet. My wife behaved as if I had slept with Konkin in the same bed all my life. What was next? Because if there was any logic to it (and a logic could be discerned there) it wouldn't be long until it revealed itself fully. What else had fate to demand of me, and what else would I have to put up with? The future seemed to hold nothing but horror.

I had to think it through, as I was not convinced that the next step might not be fatal. I couldn't just leave it to fate. I couldn't, I had no right.

However, there was no kitchen. Nor was there a corridor. There was only a pantry-like space which opened from the living room.

I came back in and switched on the light. The room was packed full of people.

They slept on two levels, with two to three in a bed. It wasn't a room at all, really, just some kind of barracks. A cooker stood by the window and there was a small dirty table overflowing with dishes. There was no cupboard or television.

'What the hell?' Voices rose from everywhere. 'Who switched on the light? Diomin, hit him on the chops. He's lost it.'

Immediately somebody hit me in the face, painfully. The light went out.

'Come,' I heard my wife whisper. 'I told you to go to sleep. So now you got it. People have work tomorrow.'

'Lucy,' I said, moving away from the snoring Konkin and leaning over towards my wife. 'Do you at least understand what is going on?'

'What?'

'It's hell, not life.' Tears were running from my eyes and blood from my nose.

'It is as it is,' my wife said. 'What are you unhappy about?'

'Lucy, we can't live like this. In the same room, all together.'

'And where can we go? Would you prefer to be on the street, in the cold?'

'But . . . Why? Can't they build their own . . .'

'From what? On what money? Go to sleep, you trouble-causer.'

She said that tenderly and I realised she thought me a fool who didn't understand what he wanted.

'And our children?'

'What? They're sleeping on the upper beds, with their children. Tomorrow you'll have to mend Verochka's bag, you'll have to get up earlier.'

'I will have to mend Verochka's bag.' That was the only clear thought in my head.

(9)

It was well past midnight when, pressing my hand to my black eye, I climbed over the snoring Konkin and crept along the plank beds towards the door. What scared me most was that somebody had hit me in the face, but I hadn't felt it as a real insult and wasn't tortured by humiliation.

The moon was bright. Shrinking from the cold, I headed up the road, barely able to understand a thing. A force was pushing me. I kept on walking until the dawn.

At midday I sat in the warm sun on a hill among the flowers and it felt good. For the first time in many, many years.

Verochka needed her bag to be mended. How would she go to school? She didn't know how to use the awl.

I'm sorry, Verochka. I smiled. I'm sorry all of you. I already knew what I had to do. I couldn't go back to trying to be somebody to them, to be somebody for them all. I was not able to think about them differently. I was trying to live for them. And only now, in the middle of the field, did I realise that I was myself here, that I was me. Me as I was. I greeted myself and grabbed myself by the shoulders. Returning to them would inevitably take me away from myself: probably for ever. That's the reason I had betrayed them, and not because I did not love them. All of them.

Of course they would be disappointed (they thought they knew me, they were waiting for me, for my hands, for my devotion, they trusted me). I would disappoint them, and they would be a little surprised, as if they had discovered something foreign and threatening under a familiar mask.

* * *

I stood up. Around me the May bees buzzed. Why hadn't I come here earlier? How strange. While I had been fighting fate in my property (losing ground inch by inch), at the same time, here, in this pure sunny clearing, there was no sign that fate existed at all. It was like I was on an altogether different plane of existence. How was it that I hadn't tried to cheat fate before, forcing my way to freedom?

I couldn't understand it. Clinging to the sparse bushes, I began to descend into the valley. I knew Verochka would be waiting for me – Verochka, my daughter Lora, my wife. They would be expecting me to turn up soon to sew the ripped school bag. Only I could do the sewing. Yes, they expected me back so that I could do many more things. And I could see, in my mind's eye, their surprised faces growing longer as slowly their faith in me weakened, their faith in my honesty and closeness to them. I could see them overtaken by a strange feeling: that I was a stranger to them. And the pit in their hearts deepened. And then, at last (and this was the most painful thing), they would understand everything. In the depths of their hearts they would condemn me. Finally, I could lean upon that condemnation; I couldn't do it any other way. Because for them I could tolerate even that existence in the barracks, but for myself – only in the grand piano room. If it had been there, I wouldn't have left, I would have stayed – with them. I wanted to be close to them, but only if I was myself. Only then.

Perhaps they were crying, back there in that stinking bear-pit. I had left them in their misfortune. I didn't want to die there with them. I knew that I was wrong; I don't renounce my responsibility, because the freedom I had gained made it worth carrying that superhuman burden.

(10)

The road descended and descended until I saw a town. It looked similar to the one I had lived in before and which I had left. Nothing surprised me. My feet took me along the familiar streets. Still not entirely sure if it was a dream or reality, I walked through a familiar doorway. When I saw the many doors, it didn't raise a joyful storm inside me as I had expected it would. But the tension that had dogged me for decades (or so it seemed) suddenly fell away. I could even recall the moment it had started, its first, as yet weak, flash: that moment in the studio when, having taken a brush into my hand I found I couldn't paint because I had noticed the grand piano in the corner of the room. I hadn't envisaged then, that that unfathomable, unfamiliar feeling that came over me was only the beginning. The beginning of something much worse.

I wandered first into the snooker room. I touched the yellow ball, frozen on the green surface. It was quiet in there. Unnoticed, I went down to the woodwork room. Perfect order ruled there; the floor was sparklingly clean, the tools were ordered in three rows on the shelves. The beautiful turning bench was pulled out into the middle of the room.

The studio stood in twilight and I drew open the blinds; diagonal rays of sunlight pierced the empty space. The colours on the canvas on the easel screamed of insanity. I lifted a tube that had fallen onto the floor. In the corner, in their usual place, stood the finished paintings, their faces towards the wall. I didn't go to look at them; it was sufficient to know that, though they hid their content, they were there.

As I climbed the stairs, the steps squeaked in the silence.

The door to the grand piano room opened without a sound, as it always had. In the half-empty room with its parquet floor, the grand piano stood in its place with the Beethoven bust upon it. There was the stand for sheet music, the small, decorated table where my father's violin lay. And, lit by the sun which streamed through the large windows, the composers' portraits gazed at me.

I had barely touched the keys when somebody knocked quietly on the door.

'Am I disturbing you?'

'No, come in.'

'You were away for so long, I thought . . .'

'No, everything is fine,' I said to her. And I felt such a sense of joy at that soft, half-forgotten distance that was present between us. 'And you? Have you been to your dressing room already?'

I needed to reassure myself, though it was perfectly clear.

She was about to leave the room.

'Lucy.' I took her hand. 'Tell me, do you remember anything?'

'What do you mean?'

'You . . .' I stepped a little closer to the grand piano. Beethoven's bust had a glued scar on its forehead. I touched the glue line and hastily removed my hand.

'It's fine.' I forced a smile. 'See you at lunch?'

'See you at lunch.' She smiled back, as she left the room.

The End

Nikodimova was sixty when she noticed the small bloody discharge. She didn't take any notice at first, but then the skin under her eyes became smoother. Just like that. She began to feel like living and enjoying herself. And the birds and spring. In the mornings, while in the shower, she discovered her body with astonishment. Not in the prime of youth, of course, her skin drooped here and there, but still, in shape, sufficiently supple.

She could reach her toes without bending her knees, the stream of water pleasantly drumming against her vertebrae and her waist, running in a warm stream down her bottom and thighs.

For a while Nikodimova refused to accept that her body had begun giving her pleasure. She had a son and a daughter who were already parents themselves. She was supposed to be a grandmother and nothing more. It was shameless to take pleasure in her sixty-year-old body in the shower. The warm water running between her breasts, across her stomach and her thighs caressed Nikodimova like a lover. Yes, her body had regained some of its former sensitivity, there was no doubt about it. It even longed for something crazy. God knows what.

Nikodimova carried on with her life, ignoring the changes, afraid of herself and of ruining the image of mother and grandmother in the eyes of those she lived for. But not long after, her daughter Marina noticed the changes in her face and gait.

'You're getting younger, Mum,' she said, a little surprised. Unpleasantly surprised. And Nikodimova grew restless, not knowing what to do. There was no need for her to look like a worn-down granny, but running around like a bride besides her daughter was indecent too.

She hid the sanitary towels she had started buying again from the rest of the world so that, God forbid, nobody discovered. It wasn't normal at sixty.

In the meantime, the wrinkles on her bottom disappeared; her breasts lifted slightly and grew firmer. Against her will, Nikodimova became seductive.

'Mum, you walk in a kind of indecent way,' her daughter remarked once, losing her patience. But Nikodimova was unaware. Her rounded hips had begun to sway all by themselves beneath her skirt, like two little watermelons side by side.

And as her back had recently arched (the shoulder blades above her hips, like two tiny wings), her movements were wonderfully graceful, and the place where the watermelons swayed attracted the eye. When Nikodimova walked down the street the men looked at her instinctively; sometimes they even stopped. Nikodimova felt sullied (though her heart would start beating wildly). At first, the men were her age or a little younger, but later even very young men began to look. Her neighbours started whispering.

'Sha . . . Sha . . . It's shameful!'

A year later she looked in the mirror and moaned. There were no wrinkles left. It was a terrible thing to accept, but she looked as young as her daughter. Fifteen years had dropped from her. It was a miracle. And her periods were as regular as they had been in her youth. Along with the pain and all the other rigmarole. The doctors couldn't explain it. They talked about the brain and hormones and things.

Nikodimova stayed a forty-year-old for a year or so, horrifying her acquaintances and relatives. She enjoyed her relative youth, but spiritually suffered terribly. Everybody gasped when they saw her. Some screamed in horror.

Not long after that, people noticed that she looked younger than her daughter. A lot younger. Her cheeks had grown pink, her eyes shone healthily, her lips smiled involuntarily. Her breasts, which had once drooped almost to her waist, had reduced to the shameful size of a young girl's, the nipples sticking out like a teenager's. Her son and daughter were speechless. Her grandchildren stared at this girl who was their grandmother. Surprise and horror shone in everybody's eyes.

Nikodimova went to the doctors again to no avail. They said some 'reverse processes' had started; her ageing mechanism was impaired. Or something like that. But they couldn't help her. So what was left for Nikodimova? Should she hang herself? Unfortunately, it wasn't a fatal illness, quite the opposite. And a man had become attached to her; he was still a youngster, younger than her son. He called her 'Lenochka' and followed her everywhere. He cried, tortured with love. She told him her age, but it wasn't a problem for him. One day, sitting in the park with him (he stalked her), Nikodimova finally realised she had lost her mind completely. She began to feel like the *'Lenochka'* the boy kept on addressing her as, the one he loved so much. As if she hadn't had children and grandchildren. And so she plunged head first into the water, forcing herself onto the boy's chest, crying, while he stroked her hands and kissed her gently, her eyes and her neck and Nikodimova fainted from the joy that flooded her. She was young! Young! She was in love! She was alive. All over again.

This couldn't go on for long; she could no longer live with her daughter, who could have passed for her mother now. Nikodimova packed her bags and went to live with the boy, Alyosha.

Even though her children were shocked at her behaviour, in the depths of their hearts they were happy when she left, even agreeing with her decision – they could no longer bear the glances and surprised cries of others. They were horror-struck seeing Nikodimova looking like a twenty-five-year-old.

She escaped to the town of K, where she lived a healthy sexual life with Alyosha, screaming every night from pure joy – a strong, real, primitive, physiological joy. Alyosha went crazy too. But not long after he noticed that Nikodimova seemed to have grown much younger. Younger than him. He struggled to find her tiny breasts in the darkness, and her hips had lost their womanly attractiveness, becoming more and more boyish. Here and there bones began protruding.

Nikodimova was confused. She cried, appalled at her skinny body, which looked like a teenager's with long, bony limbs and sunken eyes. But what could she do? Soon after Nikodimova noticed that her periods had become irregular and on one occasion Alyosha, having turned on the light, screamed in horror: an underage girl was in his bed, little more than a child, gazing at him with loyal puppy eyes.

'What's happening to you?'

'I don't know, Alyosha.' Nikodimova began to cry. 'Don't leave me, please!'

'But how can I live with you? You're just a child!'

'Please don't leave me!'

Alyosha didn't leave her, but gradually he stopped living with her as a woman. Nikodimova had shrunk so much that nearly nothing of the woman was left. The tiny breasts and hips were gone, and what was left of her woman's nature held no attraction for someone Alyosha's age or height.

Alyosha played with her for a while, getting only some fatherly pleasure from it. But finally he lost his nerve. Nikodimova was becoming a small child. Struggling to explain the situation to her, crying as he drove, he took Nikodimova to an orphanage. Soon after he married the daughter of a banker.

Nikodimova's brain was changing fast. Though she still remembered her previous life, when she was playing with the other children with building blocks she was no longer able to feel anything much of the mother or the grandmother she had been. Though it was there, it felt like some distant dream. Her tiny body had a life of its own; it had to move constantly and to be happy. And so Nikodimova ran joyfully around the garden for the whole day with the other children, had fights and climbed trees (for which she got into trouble). Somehow, she would forget who she was, enjoying her health and life to the full. Only occasionally would she stop, pierced by an arrow of consciousness; then she would look different from the other children, as if that distant grandmother Nikodimova was knocking from the past and sticking her aged hand through the door. But then, involuntarily, her attention would turn to the children running around her and any consciousness would disappear for a long time.

Soon Nikodimova was put in with the youngest children as she grew even smaller. She didn't stay there long. A year later, a special panel, after some consideration, transferred her to a home for infants. That was where very small babies and the newly born were kept. Nikodimova could barely walk; often she would fall down. A month or so later, she began crawling. Now there was nearly nothing left of her former consciousness. When she was fed from a bottle she was not able to comprehend anything. She could not recall her children or her grandchildren or Alyosha.

The strangest thing was how soon Nikodimova disappeared from the newborn baby unit. As a nurse explained, Nikodimova had looked that night like a newborn. She refused to take a dummy. The next morning, when the nurse went to her cot, it was empty.

Nikodimova had grown younger according to the normal timescale, if in the reverse direction. But from this point it became impossible to comprehend or explain. Nikodimova hadn't disappeared physically, as we might assume. Some sensations and feelings lingered within her; some flashes of consciousness remained. She couldn't see the light in the warm, comfortable sack in which she swayed blissfully to the beat of the moving creature, much more powerful than herself.

On the Road

It all started one morning. Somebody called me and told me to go down this street and that street to a particular spot. A person stood waiting for me there and instructed me to go to another spot. There another person was waiting, who, having glanced at me, showed me where I had to go next. When approaching the sixteenth spot, I suddenly asked myself, 'This is all very well, but what am I actually doing?' I had no idea why I had kept on walking, though of course, I understood that I had to do so if they had phoned me. After all, they had asked me and I had agreed. But I couldn't recall what they had actually asked me to do! They had just asked me to go here and there without providing any further explanation.

'Hello? Is that you? Could you please go there and then there . . .'

'What for?'

'It's really important! We need you to go there, please.'

That was all. I couldn't say no.

To be honest, though, I'd had my own plans that day. That morning I had been planning to go to Gavrilov's to collect some goods. I had four important things scheduled for the day and seven smaller matters. I hadn't even slept at home the night before. You have to agree it was strange and a little difficult to understand. What was I doing travelling from one place to another? I didn't know. 'Hello, I recognised you. Now you need to go down Blackearth Street as far as San Mari alley.' 'Thanks.' And off I went. The polite, serious tone with which I was addressed by my attendants forced me on and wouldn't let me go. After all, they were freezing there in the street, waiting for me! Though I didn't see the meaning of it all, I value qualities like respect and human effort. Putting such a large team of people together obviously meant something, even if I didn't understand what. For instance, if I were the only one involved, then it might have been a joke, a bet of some kind. But I assure you – I've been on the road for a number of days and have met multiple attendants. I'm hurrying to meet another now. They don't joke around., 'This way, please. It'll take you to the Three Elephant Tower.' 'Thank you.'

The longer I travel, the more I see the importance of what I am doing.

I have to admit that until the day I got that call, my life had been my own, but what had its value been? What were Gavrilov's goods worth? And those shoes that needed repairing? Of course, all that had been mine. But was any of it important?

My road, as I call it, is totally different. Though my life is no longer my own, I feel I'm doing something important here. Everything that happens is important. And to be honest, it's none of my business what it's all about. I can sense the importance of it. Something inside me has lit up.

'Hello. Thanks for coming. Now, go down New Street, as far as Triple Gate.'

'Thank you.' I'm always polite.

When you think about it – there had to be an end, and there had to be a purpose. It couldn't be that there were so many people wasting their time playing some kind of game rather than going to work. There was obviously a purpose. It would become clear soon. They had called me, not somebody else. Who am I? There, another of the attendants just gave me a hot sandwich and a cup of strong coffee from a thermos. Who would waste that kind of money on me if it wasn't serious?

'And you are . . .' I held my breath.

'They called me,' the attendant replied. 'This is my place here. I have to meet you and feed you, so that you have the energy to carry on.'

'Aha, so . . .'

I glanced at the attendant. His eyes also shone with the knowledge of the importance of what was happening.

'Where did you get the thermos from?'

'Somebody brought it to me.'

I didn't ask who. It was clear that somebody had phoned him. Somebody had bought some bread and sausage from the shop. Somebody had made a toasted sandwich. Somebody had bought a thermos. What is a piece of bread and sausage? It doesn't cost much, does it? If they call you and ask you, then why not do it? For what purpose? I don't know. Why do you always need to know the meaning of what you've been asked to do? You can do these kinds of small things without there being some kind of meaning; you don't have to go into it that deeply.

So I carried on walking. I spent the first night in somebody's flat.

'You need to get some sleep. You need the strength to carry on.'

'Thank you.'

So they took me to a flat. Before nodding off, I looked around at the unfamiliar surroundings, but couldn't work out where I was. I can't deny that I experienced a kind of fear; on the other hand, I was pleased. Yes, pleased. I was a bit dizzy from it all. A secret is quite something after all. I didn't ask any questions at the breakfast table. I could see that they valued my reserve. For some reason I was afraid to even look at them. Somehow, I didn't feel like I should.

'Help yourself to more salad.' They made sure I had enough to eat.

'Don't worry, thank you. Everything is very tasty.'

I had no doubt that they had received a telephone call too. They had gone to the place they had been told to, met me, and arranged somewhere for me to sleep. They had fed me in the morning and then showed me where to go next. It wasn't such a complicated task. Had they made some kind of big sacrifice? They hadn't really sacrificed anything, just some salad.

'Goodbye!' We shook each other's hand. The silence drew us closer, somehow.

How long had I been on the road? I found it difficult to say exactly. Although I was familiar with the town I was travelling around, everything had started to look different. When I passed the bank, I recalled that I had a tiny sum of money deposited there, but it seemed somehow irrelevant.

The people around me were the same, but I no longer lived the kind of life they did. The attendants fed me and put me to bed.

Twice a day when they met me they said, 'So, if you *need* to, you know . . . go through that arch, first door on the left.' After all, I was only human. Then they would explain where I had to go next. What did I need? When you think about it, all this stuff with the attendants in the street was only because you need to eat and sleep and wear something. They gave me a nice warm jacket recently, right there on the street; the weather had cooled down. I couldn't say that they didn't look after me. My body had everything it needed. I felt chirpy, because at noon they always offered me the chance to have a nap for an hour. If I felt I had enough energy, I said no. I tried to respond to their care with nobility. If they did so much for me, it meant my journey was important to them. I felt that they cared more about me than their own real needs. They offered me extra time to rest, even though I could feel that they needed the opposite – for me to carry on. It was I who needed the rest. So, if I was able to, I would refuse the rest.

Nobody actually forced me to do anything. I was a free person. I had left as soon as they had called me and met the first attendant, so why would I start playing with them, resting, not resting? It would have been better then to stop altogether. You need to walk with honesty, with all the strength you have.

Of course, I could have stopped. Nobody made me carry on. Nobody followed me. It took me an hour or more to travel from one point to the next. I could have left the route and gone back to my life, why not? I could have. When I recalled my life, my heart began to beat faster. My life . . . Of course, I had had a life, I had! But it was only on the road that I had begun to really feel that I had one. God knows how I had lived before. I used to get upset about the potatoes (which had begun to rot in the cellar and I hadn't noticed). That's how it had been. I would never have known what it was to really have a life, if not for the road. Now I knew. But . . . So far, I wasn't keen to go back. I was concerned that there was no secret in that life. Everything was transparent – too transparent. To be honest, I even worried that the life on the road might come to an end. I imagined approaching the next attendant and him saying, 'Thank you. That's it. It's enough. Thanks for having agreed to do what we asked.' For some reason I was afraid of that moment. Afraid to be left on my own in the world. To lose this *important* role. I knew that I was doing something important (even if I was not sure what). They needed me, they fed me, they arranged somewhere for me to sleep, they escorted me. I was somebody, that was for sure. So what if I didn't understand anything? I didn't feel less important for that; actually, quite the contrary was true! I felt that this multitude of people were looking after me. That's what I particularly valued. In my old life nobody had paid any attention to me (apart from a couple of people closest to me). Actually, I had been a nobody in my own life; that's how it seemed to me.

The most important thing, I thought, was to carry on; it was better than just living. In the other life everything was too unstructured and complicated. On the road I was focused and taciturn. Everything was simple. I was like an arrow. That's why I was afraid that, having thanked me on behalf of everybody, one of the attendants would disappear around the corner. I didn't have their address or telephone number; they had appeared unexpectedly in my life and could similarly disappear unexpectedly. Then I would be left with nothing. That was, with *my life*. I feared that moment; on my own in a foreign (that is *my*) city. Everything would close in, become too tangible, would hurt me again. Any little trifle. As it does in life. Now I was walking, and nobody could reach me. Because I was on the go. Because they met me and told me where to go next. I hoped the chain wouldn't break. Recently, I arrived at the alleyway indicated and froze; there was nobody waiting there for me. I didn't know what to do. I stood there, confused. I thought I would have to start *living* again. But I wasn't used to it anymore, and I didn't want to. What did 'to go shopping' mean? And what was it 'to call the director's assistant'? Or to 'mend socks', 'to go for negotiations', 'to knock', 'to be afraid to be late'? On the road I was never worried about being late. Nobody told me how fast to go. I just walked. And if I rushed, that was my decision, on my own incentive.

No, I just couldn't imagine that I would have to start *living* again. I felt a kind of horror; there was no other way of putting it.

On the other hand, though, what was I to do? There would be nobody to feed me, nobody to arrange somewhere for me to sleep. Life was a world of worries.

Fortunately, it just so happened that I had gone to the wrong alleyway. A block further along, I reached a crossing where an attendant was waiting for me.

'Let's go, your bed is ready.'

'Thank you. You shouldn't have gone to all that bother.'

What a sudden relief it was!

I was still a normal person though; they would put a film on for me, before I went to bed. They would switch on the evening news. I kept up-to-date with the world. But somehow, it just didn't concern me. It was like food, sleep. My brain demanded some information and it was given to me. And that felt good. I didn't feel any spiritual hunger. Occasionally one of the attendants would take me to the theatre. Once, at the end of the fifth month, I found a woman in my bed – soft and warm. In the morning she was gone. It was just a body. I had no idea if those women came to me or somebody called them. You couldn't call them a trifle; they weren't a salad or a thermos. But, as I said, I try to stay as far away as I can from any *meaning*. They looked after me in all senses. And I did what I had been asked to on the phone. Voluntarily. For some reason they needed me.

I didn't assign any particular meaning either to food or to women. Maybe it had some kind of meaning in my other life, but not on the road. On the road what was important was simply the road. On one occasion I met my wife; she didn't recognise me. And it was no wonder; I was wearing somebody else's clothes. And, I believe, a number of years had passed. She had got older. She was also *my life* . . . I was about to go up to her and hug her, but something stopped me. To hug her would have meant stopping, and not going on to the next attendant. I had been circling the same city. On my way I would bump into relatives, former acquaintances, co-workers. However, none of them would recognise me. It must be that on the road a person is different from the way they are in life; changed somehow, with a completely different inner state. They would walk past me, sometimes nudging me with their elbow. But I no longer felt close to them. They were somehow distant. While I was not *living*, they were distant to me. The worry in their eyes concerned me. They were in a rush and their eyes were full of worry. They walked, somehow, automatically. I hurried too, but inside I was pure. I wasn't burdened with meaning. They were too conscious of themselves.

I met my daughter on a bridge. I recognised her from the mole on her face and by her eyes, which were identical to mine. At first I didn't understand why she stood looking at me. I was accustomed to people not recognising me. Fear stirred in me. What would I say to her? Would I tell her that somebody had phoned me once and I had agreed to go? She wouldn't understand. How old was she? She looked almost grown-up.

I approached her because she stood where an attendant should have been waiting for me. My daughter recognised me, I realised, while at the same time not recognising me, being somewhere hopelessly distant.

'Let's go. The bed is ready.'

'Thank you. You shouldn't have bothered.'

That night I stayed in my own home. But I wasn't me. My wife and daughter fussed around me, trying to look after me. They knew, of course, who I was, just as I had known my wife when I met her in the street. But that was it. They looked at me as if they were in a dream – exactly like that. Some inexplicable coldness emanated from their eyes. A cold indifference replaced their living emotions. One more minute, I felt, and we would fall into each other's arms.

'Please, have some more salad.'

'Thanks, it tastes good.'

I recognised their feelings, but they held no power. No power over me, no power over them.

'You need to take the number eight tram up to the high school building.'

'Thank you.'

My daughter walked one way and I walked the other. I had almost reached the high school when I began to shake. I sat on a bench and began to cry. It was a good thing that there was nobody around. After I had cried, I carried on.

One day, I will hopefully reach my destination. Another attendant will take me, not to his own house, but to meet the people who phoned me. To whoever it was who called the attendants. To whoever it was who called my wife and my daughter. And they will explain everything. Those people, who took my life from me. And then . . . Then I will understand what *the road* meant and why it was needed. I will understand everything.

A.A.A.

The letter came in the morning, a month ago. It told me to choose one of the following: a broken spine, a stroke, sclerosis of the liver or an open stomach ulcer.

At first, when I started receiving the letters, I thought they were a joke. I've always believed that there is a God, of course, and that he held my life in his hands, but God had always been a kind of feeling to me. He was real in a different way to the other things in my life like my work, my family, this table, the tree outside. They were two different kinds of reality.

Ten years ago I received a very simple, stamped letter, in which, in clear language, I was told that the time had come for some positive changes to my life. I was offered a choice between: a child, winning a sum of money to the amount of five years' wages, an unexpected promotion at work, or my architectural project being accepted by the Council of International Architects in Brussels. It flustered me. I had thought that I understood the essence of fate: it chooses forms of happiness and unhappiness for you. It's terrible and at the same time very simple. If a mountain appears in the road in front of you, there's not much you can do about it. You're not God, are you? There is the mountain and there you are, at the foot of it.

But this was a different understanding of fate. As far as I understood it, my main fate-line remained, I walked the usual path. What was strange here was this – I had been granted some kind of freedom. I was given the ability to make a choice between fortunate and unfortunate events. Ten years ago, after some consideration, I chose to have a child. It was a tough decision; I really wanted my architectural project to be accepted in Brussels, I wanted to be recognised. Right from the beginning I was not tempted by the sum equal to five years' salary or promotion at work. Like anybody, I occasionally dreamed about being a millionaire and having a great career, but having a son or having my work acknowledged was more important to me. So I had a daughter. 'Birth of a healthy baby' read the third choice in the letter, signed by some 'A.A.A.'. When, as instructed, I underlined the chosen line, I had added in brackets, 'I would like a son, if possible.' But exactly nine years ago, after sending off the letter, my wife, who until then we had considered infertile, gave birth to a daughter. At first, of course, I was annoyed by the outcome, but after some consideration I calmed down. It was true, I hadn't received my request for a son. It was just that I had expressed an additional wish, that was all. And in the letter there was no indication in any way that additional requests would be granted. I had been treated more or less honestly.

So I remained a regular employee, professionally unknown, with the same comically small amount of money in my bank account. But I had a daughter. And, thank God (who else?), she was healthy, as had been promised. She would get the flu, but the letter hadn't guaranteed she wouldn't get ill or suffer a cold. 'Birth of a healthy baby' meant that she wouldn't have any serious or fatal illnesses.

What I think was, that, in some sense (a very narrow sense, of course), I was God. I had brought a new human being into existence, and, in addition, had secured the healthy physical nature of that baby. If God hands down some of his decisions, then you become him yourself, at least partially. But there was one thing that confused me, and still does: why did he communicate with me like a tax inspector would, rather than like a higher power? What I mean is that he contacted me by means of a letter. Is God able to use the services of the earthly Post Office? That was one thing. The other was, why were the letters I received so messy, humanly speaking? I had already thought about that. Take, for instance, the letter in which I was offered the choice of either my wife suffering a simple fracture of her leg, or a fire destroying all my architectural work, or a divorce from my wife or, finally, the death of a respected aunt. The letter had been typed on a basic typewriter on a crumpled sheet of paper. The typewriter tape was so faint and overused that some letters, especially the letter 'A' (a coincidence?) were barely visible. What was especially strange was that corrections had been made in blue ink, as if a normal proofreader had read the text and corrected it before sending it off. For example, in item one 'The uncomplicated fracture of your wife's leg', there were three mistakes; in the word 'your' the letter 'u' was missing, 'fracture' looked like 'tractor' and in the word 'uncomplicated' the letter 'a' (again – a coincidence?) was missing. And the whole page was like that; mistake after mistake.

How could you explain that? Was it a test of my faith? Were my mental abilities being assessed (just try and guess why it is so)? Or was it just simple carelessness on the part of the Highest Power (or powers?)? Which was scarcely credible. In any case, was it possible that the manner of the message from above had no meaning? Shouldn't all divine acts have some kind of higher meaning? If such a message came to you, delivered through the normal postal service on a simple piece of crumpled paper, coloured by a proofreader's corrections – should the things that at first glance seemed absurd not have some deep, mysterious significance?

I had noticed something: each time I was given a difficult dilemma to wrestle with. If, for instance, it had been a question of the fracture of my own leg, I would have chosen it without hesitation in order to keep my life's work safe, to protect my family from divorce, and to save my aunt, my father's sister, even though she was not terribly loved, nor frequently in touch, and was no longer young. There, though, the calculation was exact: I had to consciously decide to inflict pain and shock on my wife. Which, having no better alternative, I finally did. I based my choice on the following reasoning: I couldn't murder my aunt, who though not particularly important to me, was still my relative. The fact that the aunt would die anyway, if not tomorrow, then in ten or twenty years, was irrelevant to the decision. Let God decide in matters of life and death: he has no conscience. Forgive me, no *human* conscience (theoretically, he couldn't have, anyway). As far as our loving family was concerned, without it nothing else was important. I would save my life's work, but what would happen to my soul? Why did my wife need a healthy, non-fractured leg? Would she have preferred to get a divorce to avoid the pain and shock of a broken leg? On the other hand, I couldn't accept the knowledge that I had wasted my life from a creative point of view (with the disappearance of all my work). To have to start again from scratch at my age? It was the only one of the choices that concerned only me, my own misfortune – but what a misfortune! If it was just a case of a fractured rib or arm, I would have agreed in a blink and put up with any suffering (I consider myself a man). But this was about the meaning of my life, about me as a social creature.

So I chose 'A simple fracture of my wife's leg', based on the assumption that even if it was a painful, cruel event, it was still the only one without any fatal consequences. The aunt couldn't be raised from the dead, a family couldn't be glued together again, the work of a lifetime couldn't be raised from the ashes. But my wife's leg would heal. So I thanked God (how else should I have addressed him?) for having given me that choice, bearing in mind what could have been offered. It could, after all, have read: 'Your wife's leg fracture, which will be followed by a difficult and incurable disability'. What would I have done then? I would have gone insane.

I sent my answer back on time, of course. Having underlined the first choice, I added (even though I knew that adding anything was useless): 'Could I request, please, not the hip bone and not an open fracture.' For some reason it seemed to me that a hip fracture would be more painful than one below the knee. And, of course, I didn't really want the fracture to be disfiguring. It was like being in a nightmare. It was stupid, of course. It had been written very clearly, 'An uncomplicated fracture.' That was what was most important, not whether it was the hip or whether it was an open wound. As if 'not open', 'not hip' fractures can't be complicated and have terrible consequences, while open and hip fractures can have no particular consequences.

However, you can't change human nature; you guarantee 'a simple fracture' and he nevertheless keeps writing pointless caveats.

So I was not at all surprised when, a week after sending the letter (does it take so long to reach heaven? Stupid questions kept popping into my head), my wife was taken to the traumatology department with an open hip fracture. A receptionist informed me by phone. The bone had ripped the soft tissue and sharp endings of the bone stood out. It was horrible. How was I supposed to feel? Loss of consciousness due to the pain, heart-rending screams when consciousness was regained, a storm of tears. What was the meaning in her suffering that way? How I hated myself at that moment; my life's work, my sprightly aunt who, as if to make things worse, arrived to help and had no idea why I hated her so.

However, the sharp ends of the bones in the hip area (my wife had inexplicably fallen down the stairs at work), healed fairly simply (thanks to the surgeon) so that there was no evidence of the break visible in the X-ray. And the soft tissue healed so quickly that the doctors were surprised at her speedy recovery (though I, gazing at the sky, knew everything). The cast was taken off after two months, and six months later my wife jogged alongside me in the park, in her pink tracksuit, as if nothing had happened. And, seeing how healthy she was, I was happy in the knowledge that my work was safe, as was my family, and that my aunt was alive. I thanked God that the dilemma had been solved and that I had been given the wisdom and intuition to choose the only possible option.

I can't deny, though, that my mind was plagued with thoughts like, why did he torture me with tasks like that? And what was the purpose of the whole exercise, anyway? But then, again, all by itself (from God?) the answer would come. 'It is needed for my spiritual work; so that the spirit doesn't weaken and so that the spiritual life should shine.' Some part of my nature kept saying, 'What's the point of a difficult spiritual life?' That part of me longed for a non-spiritual, easy, pleasant life. Without effort and tension, without the heights and depths that could only be reached through the protrusion of my wife's fractured hip bones. But God didn't care about that side of human nature; he operated through the means of *fate* and *choice*. He would offer a choice and then watch: what would happen in my little soul? What powerful struggles, what motivations and so on. God the torturer? No, it's just how men are constructed: not only to stuff themselves with cake, but also to struggle with their conscience, with their brain, to growl not only with a physical stomach, but also with a spiritual one. That is how we differ from animals who are not able to shine spiritually.

How should I answer the letter, which was as implacable as it was laconic?

Please choose:

1. A spinal fracture and incurable disability (in time, the ability to move will partially return).

2. A stroke (loss of speech, memory and paralysis in the legs. Partial rehabilitation of speech and memory, full rehabilitation of the legs in the future).

3. Cirrhosis of the liver followed shortly by death.

4. An open, bleeding stomach ulcer (four complicated operations and a strict diet for the rest of your life).

Please present the answer within one month as usual.

A.A.A.

This time all four choices (why were there always four, perhaps it had some higher significance?) referred only to me, but that didn't make it any easier. I had calmed down in recent years; I had achieved a lot in my life. As an architect, I was being recognised bit by bit, we had bought a small house in the suburbs, my daughter was a real beauty. So why this again? The spiritual life? The letter again? You always got one when you least expected it. You pull it out by chance from the pile of correspondence and freeze, horror-struck in the face of fate. Why did you need to remind yourself of me, God, in such a strange way? If I have been chosen for some special purpose, why not show me a miracle, like a voice from heaven, or an unearthly, shining creature stood in the corner while I'm on my own in a room? Then, perhaps, I would begin to believe for real – not just in my brain (the letter had never lied to me), but in my heart as well. No, you had to reduce yourself to this banal state, to these mistakes and corrections in the text? Down to this appalling mechanical office style in which clerks write, not gods. But who could I complain to? I couldn't see this higher power with my own eyes. The only means of communication I had been blessed with was to send my response to God with the choice underlined. I didn't understand it at all. Why play these comedies? Why play the fool? If you are God, then you know everything, or can find it out anyway, without the Post Office's involvement. So there must be some kind of higher significance (to test my faith?) which I was not able to comprehend.

Today was the final day to send the letter. I could choose not to send it at all. That choice was open to me as well. It was not written anywhere that I must answer, that I had no right not to take responsibility for my fate. But then I would be taking an enormous risk, leaving my fate fully in God's hands. It would be better and worse at the same time – to be able to have some kind of partial power over my fate. Just think about the people who have children, receive millions in winnings and suffer fractured bones and open stomach ulcers without any influence of their own on events. (Of course, not every wish to have a child is granted). They have no idea about the balance of happiness and unhappiness (I once turned down the opportunity of winning a trophy at an international architectural competition in Zurich, which had been offered in exchange for a serious family argument). They don't have to choose the best from the good. Or the least worst from the bad. I have been granted something superior, in that I can have a partial influence (within a narrow frame) on the highest decisions related to my fate. I can always avoid the worst: though it takes a long time to decide what the worst really is. But that was only the other side of the privilege that was granted to me, for what merit I'm not sure. And I not once – not once – used the choice not to choose (in fear that if I didn't intervene, I would get an unacceptable choice). I understood that in being given the right to make these incredibly important choices, the choices tied me. I not only gained freedom, but lost it too. To the extent that freedom is irresponsibility. From the day I received the first letter, I became partially responsible. By what means did I pay for the chance to change my fate? With my irresponsibility. With the childishness of the soul.

Special notice should be taken of my last case. If I didn't reply that day, it would mean that I surrendered fully to the will of God (or gods – A.A.A. – one God in three persons?). Which would mean that possibly, as promised, I would die soon of cirrhosis of the liver. And I still had so much left to do in life. The only way (granted me) to avoid that fate was to send the letter with a different choice underlined. But which one? A spinal fracture and incurable disability? A stroke and speech and memory loss with paralysis to begin with? A bleeding stomach ulcer and four serious operations (and, if I understood it correctly, the removal of the major part of the stomach)? They were all terrible. All. But one of the choices would be realised. If only I could choose, not between these four misfortunes, but between unhappiness and happiness! Or at least, I could think of a fifth misfortune that would have suited me better. No, fate did not offer me that choice; that is, to choose heaven and a life without fate, that is without trials (especially unwelcome ones).

Which meant that I had to choose from what was available. I chose an open stomach ulcer, simply because it was the only choice that wouldn't have too many painful consequences. It would mean that I did not have to carry the burden of fate to the end of my days. I was worried by the vagueness of the terms of the first choice (the spinal fracture) like 'incurable disability', 'partial recovery of the ability to move'. What did that mean? Would I be restricted to a wheelchair then? Or would it be crutches? In the second choice (the stroke) it spoke about a 'full recovery of the function of the legs' but then on the other hand, the 'partial' rehabilitation of speech and memory. How to interpret that? That I would mumble, mutter and stutter? That I would remember who and what I was just once a week? No thank you. So what was left? Cirrhosis of the liver had already been discounted, as I mentioned before, because it meant an early death. So only the open stomach ulcer was left. Which was a nightmare too – especially when I thought about how I would have to endure four serious operations (I could just imagine how much suffering I would have to go through). But the consequence – a strict diet until the end of my life – was not the worst thing imaginable. A restricted diet, even if it was strict, was not the same as being confined to a wheelchair or losing my life. I thought that perhaps one choice had been offered which was easier, a 'more acceptable' option (as otherwise the choosing would have been impossible), but it had been concealed so that I had to make an effort to seek out the best decision.

'Kolya, what's taking you so long?'

'I told you – just a minute. Wait.'

My wife and daughter had no idea. Nor did my respected aunt. I would underline choice number four (a bleeding stomach ulcer) and would add (as I always did, not able to restrain myself), 'Please could I have the ulcer without the perforation of the stomach wall?' I would seal the envelope and run to the postbox. I knew the address: 16 Green Street, flat 63. The address was in my town. I had, of course, checked the address a long time before; there was no such house, nor any such street. But the letter would get there. As they always had.

My stomach growled happily, still healthy, and I stroked it gently and sadly. Sorry.

Sooner or later, I knew I would receive a letter with the choices: '1. Death; 2. Death; 3. Death; 4. Death'. And with a joyful giggle, I would tear the letter to pieces.

The Author

When a writer decides to make his protagonist a writer, you can only pity his poor dried-up imagination. But the author who dreamt me up as a writer is still writing, bent over his desk – now he is an author. He is in the process of creating me – and I can speak, move, and think. The fact is that I am painted. But at the same time, I am me, fully alive, with a family, a home and so on. I truly am alive, but at the same time (and I understand this perfectly) I am nobody. I am, if you will, the fruit of an author's imagination. But I insist that just because of that, it does not mean that my existence stops being mine: it is still real and, in some ways, unique. So now, for example, I'm here drinking a coffee. Should I doubt the taste of this drink? Does this cup (which is small, brown, smooth and warm) not actually exist? Because, actually, what is this reality we are talking about? The fact that the author has his own reality, doesn't mean that mine diminishes. I would even suggest the contrary. The more creative the author is, there, in his reality, the more alive I become.

To tell you the truth, I don't feel like I'm a picture. I live a full life. My children are just as worthy as any others, as is everything else in my life. It even seems at times, that it's the author, in fact, that doesn't actually really exist. Because, when it comes down to it, where did I get the idea from that I'm his creation? That I don't have an independent existence? Well it was, how should I put it? It was a hunch. I was scribbling something down once and suddenly realised that I (including everything I was writing) was, at that very moment, being created. Honestly, the thought horrified me. But no. I do believe my own eyes and ears; look, I can see them there, in the mirror. They're watching and listening. But on the other hand, if you think about it, can you actually really trust them? Those eyes and ears of yours? I've noticed that many people really do trust them. When a person walks down the street, they really do believe that they exist, and that they haven't just been made up by somebody.

I'll explain using my own writing. I'm sitting here writing – my hero is walking along a street. He's a university professor. He's just given a lecture on psychology (he's a Doctor of Psychology). So, as he walks along, I write about where he goes, how he rushes, about his feelings, his worries and so on. In general, the story rolls along all by itself: the plot, the denouement, you understand? And then suddenly it hits me: my character is alive! It's true. He is living there, somewhere: well, in my imagination, where else? Obviously. But he thinks that he is alive on his own merits. And this realisation threw me into a state of confusion; I might equally have been created by somebody else and just believe, like my character the professor, that I have this independent existence. So I eat, drink and scribble, I have children and raise them. In other words, I live. But then my character lives too.

Another thought stopped me in my tracks: if some reader is going to follow my protagonist, does that mean a reader will start to read about me too before long? About all my thoughts and feelings? It's entirely different, I think you'll agree, to have a private life while at the same time you know that, perhaps, when you're thinking about something intimate, there is somebody there, in this other reality, who experiences this intimacy of yours. It's not that it's an entirely negative feeling, per se (it's quite a nice idea to be in somebody else's world), but, on the other hand, it's not too pleasant, either. Because you have all kinds of thoughts. The thoughts I have occasionally! Sometimes during the night, sitting quietly at my desk reading a rough draft of my work, I swear I start to think I'm some kind of genius. Seriously. For God's sake, this is real, these thoughts, this imaginative flight, this is real style. And what, essentially, is the difference between this and what the classic writer K wrote, or the classic writer N? Is my writing worse than theirs? It's just that they lived years ago and a lot of time has passed. Once, that classic writer K would have sat, just like I am today, looking at his unpublished manuscript, which nobody had labelled a classic yet, being just a nobody, an unknown writer: in other words a total nobody in society's eyes. There he sits, torn by doubt, when suddenly it occurs to him that his writing is, for God's sake, it is . . . Well, it's clear what he's thinking. And then some time goes by, the present turns into the past and everybody knows that in the past even a bowler hat or a fan is a 'classic', or interesting; it's the past, isn't it? The lovely, lovely past. And we're not just talking about a bowler hat here – we're talking about the archives of the writer K; there are some deep thoughts, and the feelings he expresses are truly noble. And his imagination. And his endless searching. His courage. It's really deep, isn't it? And in addition, he used to hang around with the classic writer N. Just think about that. They lived together once, in that past.

So sometimes you sit there by yourself thinking about this great writer K who, for goodness' sake, wasn't considered a classic writer at all when he was alive, but was half-forgotten, an unacknowledged literary figure like myself today. For example. So it's quite logical to think that tomorrow I will be a 'classic writer'. No, I'm serious. They will publish my diaries and my letters. They will collect everything that I've written, searching for even the smallest article in a magazine. Even the diaries of so-called ordinary people are published: everybody's interested to know how people lived a hundred years ago. In a hundred years' time I'll also be antique, won't I? I would be interested to read the letters of an ordinary cook if she lived, say, in ancient Greece. And in 2,000 years I'll be, you have to admit, incredibly ancient to somebody.

Sometimes you get so carried away sitting in your armchair (with the night dark outside the window), it's as if it has already happened. And you don't even consider that somebody is happily *reading* your thoughts, in the direct sense of the phrase. And that's just an example; that's the kind of thought that suddenly comes to a person.

Let's say somebody laughs at me, thinking 'Oh, look at him, who is he trying to be? Look at him, what a genius!' The only thing that makes me feel a bit better is that as they sit there in their chair, reading about my life, they might well laugh – but they don't know me, and that's what is important. Though my name would probably be mentioned and stuff, but what's in a name? It's just a word. It's not the same thing as me. There might be other people with the same surname. And also, where is he reading me? Who is he? What world does he live in? All I know is that there is an author and a reader and me, the picture, and all of us, though connected somehow, live in different worlds.

The author, for instance, who is he? Where is he? I have no idea. I wrote a novella and sent it to a publisher – there were all kinds of negotiations, successful, not successful. Which is understandable. If you get published, you look forward to there being some kind of response. It happens or it doesn't. If it does, it's not necessarily the way you expected. You get misunderstood and so on: the usual stuff. To sum up, that's the life of a literary figure – imagining the kind of recognition he will get tomorrow and how he sees himself. But now it is the way it is. And then also, there are my children, my two little daughters, and my wife. Just as it should be. And then there are all the everyday issues in life, the money problems. That is my world. For better or worse, it belongs to me. So where does the author fit into all this, the one who is creating me and my life? And the reader who reads about that life?

They both exist. I understand that too. But they exist in their own worlds. Like my hero the professor, rushing home after his lecture, who is in his own world. You've got to agree it's good that our paths don't all cross (though sometimes we release each other into the world), otherwise I wouldn't be able to bear the thought that somebody was in my thoughts and feelings. But if you are on a different plane, then why not? If I won't meet you in my little world, you can stay in it as long as you wish. It's even better for me, knowing that I am not alone. It's even better to know that I am created, honestly. Firstly, my soul feels somehow calmer. At times you come home, depressed, beside yourself. You don't know what to do. You run backwards and forwards like mad trying to achieve something. Then you sit and think, maybe you should have done more? Have you done something wrong? You have doubts, you despair and have mad outbursts. You get into such a state sometimes, honestly; it's like you're being crushed by fate. What's that all about? *Brrr*!

And at that kind of moment you slap yourself on the forehead and think, why did I fall into such a state of hopelessness, I'm just a picture! The writer knows what the future holds for me, so it was he who made me do what I've done so far. Everything that happens to me is all a part of the plot, isn't it?

I know from my experience how it is. For instance, my hero, the professor. I absolutely know what he is thinking and feeling when he walks home. I can see right through him; his quiet, happy family life, his creative urges, his self-reproaches. 'So how come, having had such dreams of being an independent thinker, you became a university lab-rat, you son-of-a-bitch! You rush to meetings with your knees trembling in front of the Dean!' That's how my hero, the professor, talks to himself as he walks home after his lectures. All of these kinds of feelings flash through his mind. When he gets home, the news will be awaiting him that his daughter has fallen ill and has been rushed into hospital. He has no idea yet, only I know about it. And, in advance, I worry about him, honestly, like I would worry about a close friend, because I know what's awaiting him in half an hour, buried as he is in his problems. It can't be any other way. That is the logic of life and that is the way that a character has to be revealed. And so, I imagine, the professor gets home, and his wife is in the doorway, in tears.

'Katechka is in hospital!'

Well, the professor's heart goes thump, thump thump.

'What happened?'

'I don't know, she fainted in the kitchen. I managed to revive her. The doctor said it's something to do with her heart.'

'Her heart? It can't be. Where is she now?'

I'm not going to tell you what happened next – I'll leave you to imagine how the professor's life is turned upside down. For a while, the unhappiness he has felt that he hasn't become some kind of second Sigmund Freud evaporates from his head. Something very different starts to torture him. He loves his Katechka so much! Now that his daughter is in hospital, he remembers how, when she was still a toddler, she used to come running towards him shouting, 'Da-d-dy!' and would throw herself into his arms. He remembers the suitcase full of presents he had bought for her stood next to them.

As I have already said, I'm not going to start telling you what and how he feels. In short, it's about a person's character, his fate and all that. And there he is, the professor, up to his ears in his little world, drowned by the feelings that flood him. That's how it is. It's exactly how I feel, when some kind of misfortune overtakes me. But will he shake his head? Will he remember, as he sees his wife crying in the doorway, that he's just a creation? That this is all just a work of creation?

No, he won't. He'll probably start banging his head against the wall, or just slump down on a chair in the kitchen, distraught.

Here's another example. Quite often somebody bumps against you in the street. It's no big deal, is it? Or someone shouts at you for no reason. All sorts of feelings start to bubble up inside you. How seriously we take everything that happens to us – our sense of self-worth, the offence and everything. It's understandable. But then, what is self-worth? What are our feelings? And why, at the end of the day, is the professor a professor, not a cobbler?

And then, if you think about it, these feelings, this personality of the professor was created by me. That was my plan. And all these problems and the rudeness in the street, they are there so that I can picture him as a well-rounded person. To show that he is alive, that his nerves are alive, that his reactions are alive. The professor gets annoyed, of course, because he – a professor – was pushed by somebody who didn't apologise. And he gets annoyed with himself, because it's just a triviality he shouldn't pay any attention to. It's a weakness to get upset about such trifles. So then the professor is upset that he is so weak.

And again, when these feelings overwhelm the professor, he doesn't think, 'Look, it's true I got upset and I can't do anything about it, but maybe that's how it should have been.' In other words, he should have realised that he was in the process of being created.

What a relief it would have been for him! If the character (this fictional character) was created with these feelings, who could blame him for them? The professor's life is his and yet, somehow, not his at the same time. That's how it is!

The author exists. The author paints the portrait, colouring it with all sorts of feelings, and then he tortures it. The portrait, instead of realising that he is being created moment by moment, lives like a blind man, taking his feelings too seriously. Really. It's not wise, foolish even, not to see – not to realise – that everything is necessary and there is meaning in everything – for the author.

I am not saying, however, that I understand what the meaning of someone creating me as a writer was, or why they assigned me the thoughts I have and not others. And also, why I have two daughters rather than two sons. Why I'm married, for goodness sake! Why I was not created the king of Sweden.

But what's the point of such pointless questions? Questions like, why are you not who you are? A person can't be everything at the same time, can he? If you have been created – that is, conjured from non-existence – then it means you came in a certain body and with certain physicality and personality and a particular shape. No one can appear on the earth without these qualities, that would be non-existence. Nothing would happen. But you have been created and are being created. And I think you should be thankful for that, instead of moaning that you're not Freud.

It's okay to be upset, but the most important thing is to understand that your life-experience has been created and has its own particular meaning. For instance, the fact that my professor was upset about getting a spot on his suit (which, in fact, happened), had a particular meaning. I record these experiences so that nobody doubts my professor is real. He is a living person to me. You might wonder, why I should have written that? But everything is important: everything has meaning to a living person.

Now, I'm being clever, aren't I? Putting my jumper on, I lean over my desk. My family get on with their lives behind the door. Life goes on. Obviously. And I keep writing, creating. Just because I know that I'm a writer, sat here in my office, does it mean that I should forget that I am just a creation?

My wife enters.

'Sorry, Kolya, where are the matches?'

That's a real wife for you, and a real micro-problem. Should this make me forget that I'm a creation, and that I'm in the process of being created? Along with my wife, and my office and my writing? That table and in fact the whole country has all been created. That's clear without me having to say it, in my opinion.

When I see my colleague, who is a novelist too, let's call him S (what's the difference?), all kinds of feelings overtake me. But again, all this has been created: our meeting in the café by the metro station, and his, 'Hey, old man, your writing's not bad, honestly, not bad,' and my embarrassment (how do you respond to a comment like that?) – it has all been created. Everything. I'm positive. I walk out into the street with him; what will I do? Where will I go now? How will I say goodbye to him? I don't know yet. And I think that I'm in control of my next step, that it's my choice, my freedom. I will say goodbye as I wish. Will I really? I will do and say what is *necessary*. Yes. I will do what I am supposed to do.

My acquaintance walks away, and the trolleybus drives off. This is all being created – everything. Which is what is so breathtaking. Everybody is alive, not dead; the living suffer, they fight, they fall into a state of hopelessness. And I'm living. But everything has been created, everything. All this life has been created.

Because of this, honestly, it makes me laugh when they write about some president in the newspaper, or the economy, or some national dilemma, or negotiations. I'm telling you, everything has been created. Civil wars, coups, 'witnesses', 'historical facts'. Of course, I wouldn't be capable of creating all of that – in all that detail. But I'm the author of the reality which my professor of psychology experiences. I created him as fully rounded a character as I could. But in the reality where I live (with all its presidents, its wars and this current moment in history), in this reality I am being created along with everything that is going on around me. The power of the author who created all this, you need to understand, is of a totally different type to mine. I'm not capable of controlling more than three or four characters at the same time, let alone history with all of its politics – that's too much for me, I would give up straight away. But somebody is successfully creating us. But for me (I won't hide it) it's much more important to know that I am being created. That's how it should be. Why should I care about history? It's the backdrop for my existence. Sometimes I even question the author as I'm sat at my desk at night.

'Who are you? Where are you?'

And if you can imagine, there he is, the author, sitting at his table having created a character, who was also sitting at his desk at night asking in the darkness, 'Who are you?', 'Where are you?' – then it's like some kind of nightmare, isn't it? And that's what it is. What do my questions and my feelings mean? They are also the fruit of the imagination of the author creating me. And if I, let's say, should put into my professor's head the suspicion that I have created him and that he is not just himself, the professor will start talking to me in his thoughts. And what will that feeling be that the professor has, that he is just a character, if not my own imagination at work?

It's a nightmare, isn't it? In fact, the character has nothing of his 'own' and he can't have it. If he gets some ideas about the author, then that would be the author himself that had created that thought. It's terrible!

But what to do?

It's like a *draught*. I, the author of the professor and his feelings, am being created too. And my own feelings and thoughts, though I cling to them tooth and nail, are not mine at all. I experience them, but that is entirely different. Not everything we experience in life is ours. There you go. What can we say then about the professor's thoughts and feelings?

But a real nightmare might start if my professor, after his daughter has recovered, went back to his bitter meditation about Freud and started to write something himself. That is, my character, who, so far, has simply been living and not creating, starts to write. Now, I think you would have to agree, you might as well just throw your hands up in the air. The point is you can't change anything; the logic of the plan requires this. The *draught*, as I call it, must blow through fully. You can't stop the professor from creating a character of his own. So what am I supposed to do now? Am I going to have to write my book and the professor's book as well? It's not a problem for me to write for myself, as my personality and character spontaneously express themselves, but if I have to write for the professor too? I wouldn't be able to write for him like I do for myself. He's a professor of psychology, right? Then he, let's say, is an expert in a person's psychology, but what about his writing skills, his style? Of course, he wouldn't be able to write very skilfully, unless he possessed some real calling. In other words, I would have to write for the professor bearing in mind all the nuances of his biography and personality.

And here is the professor's protagonist – a young girl – Ala. She has a boyfriend who is eventually unfaithful to her. Actually, it's a pretty banal story. As I portray the professor as 'real', attempting to create a living character, someone alive, a personality, it's no wonder that the professor's Ala and Dima turn out quite lifelike too. It's just me, in fact, who is creating all this. And the assumption that the professor finally turns out to be a talented writer is necessary for me to show that this world created by the professor, the world of Ala and Dima, shouldn't be written schematically, and illiterately; the *draught* would be choked otherwise.

No. Ala and Dima should be so alive that their lives look no less real than mine or my professor's.

Now, here's the final problem for me to solve. Let's say Ala, to whom Dima is unfaithful, begins, in despair, to start to write. So a new world emerges. The professor creates Ala, and Ala, without any suspicion of the professor's existence, creates a heartbreaking story about Robert and Euridike's love. In general, the *draught* makes sense. My head spins, looking into the abyss, as I can't create for Ala, I don't have enough energy left. But the professor is closer to her.

Now, imagine that the stories of the professor, Ala and Robert unfold in the same city where I live, and in the same time period. Will we meet or not? It's impossible! Each of us has our own reality, which seems to be the only one.

You will not meet your author, that's for sure. You can scream or beg, but he'll stay silent. He doesn't speak *to* you, he speaks *through* you, in your thoughts and feelings. You suddenly realise that you are being created, and you scream into the starry sky, 'Where are you?' 'Who are you?' And that feeling of yours – that scream of yours – that, too, has been created, at that very moment.

Thanks to your insight, thanks to your cry, the author can manifest himself. Thanks to your picture, he can understand himself. And is it worth shedding tears that I am, it seems, nobody; that I have no 'independent' life?

Would You Forgive Me?

He got in through the window when we were sleeping with the intention of robbing, or even killing us. I was not even fully aware of what I was doing when I pulled the trigger of the pistol, aiming it at his head. He was a criminal.

But then, to have to watch the dying convulsions of the person you have shot in your bedroom – well, you understand. As if on purpose, he took a good half an hour to die, rattling and crying, all blood and froth. My wife's eyes were popping out, her face all green, she was sweating and screaming (not even able to shout any longer). The children stood in the doorway, red-faced from their deafening squeals of horror.

I ran out into the yard in my underpants, otherwise I would have gone mad. Level eight, or something like that, of the irritation of my nervous system. Why in the hell did he climb through my window?

The police and ambulance took him away. Now I could happily get on with my life with my wife and children. We threw away the carpet with the patch of blood on it. To the devil with it. But still, something was wrong. At night I lay down next to my wife, but she would pull away from me.

'What is it?' I say.

And I move closer to her. And she, unconsciously, pushes me away again.

'Liuba, what is it?'

And I move closer. On the verge of hysterics, she hisses through her teeth, as if to herself,

'Murderer!'

I am astounded. Honestly.

'Get up!' I say. 'I don't understand.'

She is afraid. Of me.

'I don't understand.' I say. 'Did you want him to rob us, to kill us?'

'But perhaps he wouldn't have killed us,' she says. 'He would have just robbed us.'

What a fool.

'Maybe,' she says, 'he would have taken something and left. But now . . .'

'Now what?' I ask, barely able to control myself.

'And now he is dead!' She screams and shouts.

My God! So that's what it is. It seems I killed a man. I'm a murderer, a villain.

'I do understand, Vitechka,' she says, twitching with sobs. 'You defended us. But why in his head?'

'I don't understand!' I shout.

'When I remember how he was dying,' she says. 'The poor thing, right here. Dying and crying. Oh! I can't anymore!'

And she bursts into tears again. I see the children standing in the doorway, watching and trembling with fear.

'Out! Go to bed!'

I felt like killing myself or somebody else. It wasn't possible to carry on like this.

So I went to his house, with the intention of examining myself; to see what a villain I was. His old mother, so like my mother, as misfortune would have it, was sitting there dry-eyed. She held on to his dead hand. Like in a nightmare. And there were his children, a boy and a girl, orphans now. The girl, the younger one, was crying, while the boy was standing with such a look on his face, that I will remember it until the last moment of my life. Suddenly the girl spoke through her tears.

'My daddy, dearest!'

But her father had two dots on his forehead.

'Dad-dy, get up, daddy!'

It was obvious she loved him. A little girl with a red, swollen nose, no more than a toddler. I staggered out, holding on to the wall. What was all this? I couldn't get my head around it. What kind of a person was I? What was I supposed to have done then? He looked so innocent, lying there like an angel. A son, a father. One of God's children. When he had climbed in through my window wearing a mask, he had simply been a criminal. Just a burglar who had got a bullet from me. A piece of filth who had dared to intrude into the peaceful life of a stranger. And that thought made me want to kill another couple of his like in my bedroom, so that the kids of scum like him could screw up their little faces, pleading for their daddy to rise up from his coffin.

I sat down on a bench in the children's playground by the house. Good God, what had I done wrong? What? I had never harmed a fly before. And then he broke into my house, my life, and now he was gone. So what had I done wrong? Why was I suffering?

Talking to myself like this, it seemed to me that I was absolutely right. But then I remembered the voice of the little girl, the toddler.

'Daddy! Daddy! Please get up!'

I was a real bastard, Liuba was right. A murderer. I had probably saved Liuba and my children from death, but I was still a murderer. Liuba was scared to touch me. Oh yes, I could walk with my head held high; not many people have killed somebody. And I have.

At that point, horror-struck, I realised I would never be able to wash the spot out. I was a killer. I would die a murderer, the sin weighing upon my soul. The sin? The thought drew me up short. For God's sake, what sin had I committed? What had I done wrong?

I sat on the bench next to their house until they took him out: the son, the father and the burglar. I heard a scream; his mother broke down weeping. Her pain was enough to drive me out of my mind.

'My little son. My little son!'

It was unbearable to listen to. She could barely walk. She had given birth to him, she had raised him. I sat there and tears the size of peas ran down my face. I didn't understand. I didn't understand anything at all. And then an intelligent-looking young man came up to me.

'It's better that you go,' he said quietly.

He looked me straight in the eyes. But, God, what was this? This brother, or relative, or whoever he was, obviously acknowledged my right to defend myself and everything but, still, he blamed me. Only me. As if to say, 'Listen, you were within your rights mate, but now go, get out of my sight. Don't hang around here, you murderer.'

What was this all about? I left, feeling like a beaten dog. There were cries, screams. His little children were shouting, his son as well now, broken-hearted. His mother was sobbing. Oh my God, what had I done? All on my own. With this hand of mine.

I went to calm down in a café. Now he was being lowered into a hole. Well . . . What could I do now? Had I been aware what I was doing when I grabbed the pistol from the drawer? He was coming towards me with a knife. It could be, of course, that he didn't intend to kill us. He probably just wanted to scare us, to make me lie back quietly in bed while he was emptying our drawers. Then . . . Now I understood Liuba. For God's sake, it would have been better to let him rob us and clear off rather than do what I did. We would have been a little poorer (and even then, the police might well have recovered everything), but at least in my chest everything would have been as it used to be. And now?

When I went home, Liuba wouldn't say a word to me. How could I live like this?

'Liuba,' I said. 'Listen! Speak!'

But instead of an answer – silence.

'Speak or I'll hit you!'

The look she gave me!

'Why are you staring at me? A murderer? Yes? You see a murderer?'

'Yes!' she said her voice trembling, on the verge of tears.

She ran out of the kitchen to sob in the bedroom. I began smashing up the dishes and the furniture. I broke the stool, the table and then fell down right there on the floor, scraping my arm, blood running everywhere. What could I do? Liuba's sobs were growing louder. The children, thank God, were at nursery school. I felt like I was going mad. I jumped up suddenly. Liuba, seeing me, darted to the corner, totally hysterical, her eyes huge, totally crazy.

'Don't kill me!' she shouted.

Well, I thought, here we go. Not far from a mental asylum now. My nerves were ragged. I turned around without a word, took a half-litre bottle of vodka from the cupboard and had a drink from it.

It was this that saved me. I knew I was behaving like a hopeless drunkard, but I pressed it to my lips and emptied it all. Ten minutes later I fell to the floor. Of course, a sedative would have been a better idea. A simple dose of Temazepam. But we had never had anything like that in the house.

Anyway, I had to find some way of relaxing. Otherwise my nerves would have come unstrung and I've no idea how all this would have ended then. So getting drunk was wise.

Liuba kept her hysteria going in the bedroom (she told me later that she had blocked the door with a wardrobe to stop me from getting in, though she knew she was being silly). She just wanted to frighten herself. Later, when everything had calmed down, she relaxed a little. Her hysteria evaporated. She moved the wardrobe back and went to the kitchen to have a look. I lay there, twisted up on top of debris. She began to scream, of course, thinking I had killed myself. Then she discovered the empty bottle and understood. I was sick a couple of times, lying there out of my mind, though I don't remember a thing.

Then I slept for about thirty hours. I woke up in my bedroom and smiled. I felt, somehow, right in my soul. Sun streamed through the window. Then Liuba came in.

'Well, how are you?' She leaned in close to me. God! Everything would be okay again. I still remembered that something terrible had happened, but I saw it now through a kind of filter. A distance had emerged. My nerves had calmed, and the sharpness of the sensation had gone. Liuba too, leaning towards me, was different now. She must have had a good sleep, too. Time had passed.

A year later, I had forgotten about it all. The idea that I had suffered for being a murderer surprised me. An unpleasant feeling remained, but there were no memories of the man dying in our bedroom. The other family accepted and grew accustomed to living without their son and father. For a time the mother would stand there, alone, lost in memory, and so would the little girl with her swollen, red nose. But later those images disappeared too. One time, walking by their house, I happened to see the mother quarrelling in a petty and angry manner with her neighbour. And I felt nothing positive or noble towards her.

Recently Liuba and I have been quarrelling over any little thing. We have more money, but the happiness is gone. Our eldest, Vova, stays out late, sometimes not coming home at night. There's an emptiness to the way Liuba behaves with me, I've noticed.

'Take out the rubbish,' she says, as she scrubs something in the kitchen. 'The Jelizarovs are flying to Paris this week.'

She would have really liked to go to Paris.

'Liuba,' I say.

'What?' She always sounds so annoyed.

'Nothing.' And I take out the rubbish.

Good God, what a life. What was happening now? Were we getting bored of each other, or something? The rubbish. Vovik. Paris. Money. Also, I had murdered somebody. Yes, it had happened. It was work the next day. I was tired. Beyond that I felt nothing. There was no meaning. During those terrible days I had felt fully alive, my emotions bubbling. And I had cried. From the pain in my heart, feeling for that elderly mother. And I had suffered.

'Liuba,' I said that evening. 'Do you still remember all that?'

'What?'

'When I killed somebody.'

'What else could you have done? Wait until he killed us?'

She tapped her spoon on the plate nervously, thinking about something else.

'I'm a murderer, aren't I?'

'Stop it, you behaved like a man.'

Which was pleasant to hear, of course. And then she said, suddenly, 'Fix the tap in the bathroom. It's taking quite a while.'

'Why are you so angry?'

'Because my life is so good.'

'So what is missing?'

'I have everything.'

What a lovely conversation.

I went to visit his grave. I felt a kind of sadness. I thought that perhaps it might move something in me. I would remember him dying in front of me. Perhaps something would tremble in my soul. But no. Apart from a cross that leaned to one side and a gravestone on which was written, 'Genadij Konstantinovich Pavlov', I saw nothing. There was some grass and, under the soil, bones.

I put an end to your journey in this world, my friend. Would you forgive me, perhaps?

It Never Ends

The film started at nine-twenty and by nine-thirty there were only about ten eccentrics left in the auditorium. To be honest, who would want to watch a film that seemed so pointless and had no plot? A girl came home from the shops and argued about something with her mother on the phone. The conversation went on for twenty minutes and the audience left. To be fair, during that twenty minutes the girl went to the toilet, saying into the phone, 'Wait a second, Mum, I need to go.' (Which livened the scene up a bit). Otherwise, nothing special happened. I stood up too and left. Who wants to worry about other people's difficulties and problems?

As I strolled home along the empty streets, I thought about the peculiarities of contemporary cinematography (the so-called *avant-garde*). After dinner and a bath, and in order to relax, having looked through an interior design magazine and having read three poems by Baudelaire (my norm for the day), I went to bed at midnight. However, at three a.m. I opened my eyes and sat up: I couldn't work out what had happened. Some vague anxiety made my heart ache. Through the window the dead city shone pale in the moon light.

What was it? Why was I not sleeping? I began to sift through all my problems in an attempt to understand the worry that flooded me. My wife would be coming back from her business trip the next day. In the evening, my daughter, currently relaxing at the sanatorium, would call me. No, that wasn't it. There were no issues at work at that moment either, just the ordinary mess.

I swung my feet off the bed and it suddenly came to me: I had been unconsciously thinking about the girl who had been trying to prove something to her mother over the phone. It was definitely she who was at the root of my anxiety. How idiotic! I had never seen a more ridiculous film. What had she been talking about? She had said something along the lines of, 'No, Mum, you don't understand how important it is to me, you don't want to understand me.' And her mother said to her, 'Liz, you've got everything you need: a man, a job. Everything will fall into place bit by bit. By the way, yesterday Nora Iljinichna dropped in. Can you imagine, they stole her new rug, right from her balcony!' But Liz snapped back, 'Mum, you're not listening to what I'm saying! I must go to Spain. It's now or never.'

She had talked about Spain and about money. I went out onto the balcony to have a cigarette.

It made me wonder; since when had I started worrying about the protagonists of the films I had seen? Down below me, an advert for the agency 'New World' was flashing, while a little further along was the sign for the cobbler's shop, a silly shoe with a shiny cat sticking out.

But where had I watched that dreadful film? In vain I tried to remember the cinema. Having had nothing to do, I had wandered into an old quarter of the city and found myself in front of a cinema hoarding. It had a pretty decent title: *The Chopped-Up Girl and the Stool with a Pentagram.* After a slight hesitation, I had gone into the old, cool building, which smelled of mould, in the hope of exciting my exhausted brain with something cannibalistically horrible, with the kind of fright-flick that was popular in cinemas like that. It was a self-service cinema with just a machine at the door, so there was nobody to ask what type of film it was.

Since when had I bothered my head about cinemas in the outskirts of the city? I threw the cigarette butt down into the street below. It was quite stuffy. Then, impulsively, I decided to go out for a walk. Yes, at three-thirty in the morning. I knew I would not be able to get to sleep anyway.

I don't recall, now, how long I wandered along the cobbled streets. My footsteps echoed in the night's silence. Suddenly, I realised I was standing right in front of the same hoarding. The silence rang in my ears. I decided to go in, as fate seemed to have drawn me to that cinema (I was still not sure which part of the town it was in).

As before, the entrance hall stank of mould and the lamp shone dimly above the door to the main auditorium. A flickering light seemed to be coming from inside. Attempting to suppress a feeling of misgiving, I put a coin into the machine and the turnstile let me in.

I entered the completely empty auditorium, attempting to not look at the screen. It was only when I sat down in the middle that I allowed myself to look up at the screen. It was the same girl on the screen. She was sleeping, curled calmly into a ball, her quilt tucked up under her chin. A clock was ticking on a side table.

I was impressed. I had never seen that before. It was cool. They were still showing the same cheap film, it seemed, and possibly didn't intend to finish until the morning.

The girl was breathing deeply and twitched in her dream. How long was she going to lie like that? Probably until seven or eight in the morning, depending on where she worked and how long she had to travel to get there.

It felt as if somebody had chained me to my seat in the auditorium. I wanted to wait until the end and make sure that she got her six or seven hours of beauty sleep, then watch as she stretched and got up. I sat as if mesmerised, unable to take my eyes off her. Minutes melted one into another.

Occasionally she moved. Three times she turned over and finally lay on her stomach.

At six a.m. sharp, the alarm clock rang and I jumped. The girl quickly got up, slapping her palm on the alarm button.

To my surprise, and with a degree of pleasure, I noted she had no nightie on. After yawning and, as I had foreseen, stretching, she went to the bathroom. Before that, though, she went to the loo. There she groaned for a long while, then stood up finally, flushed the water and yawned sweetly again.

In the bathroom she got into the shower, rubbing her whole body zealously from head to toe. Finally, she washed her hair, snorting like a horse after rain.

That was all I had time for. I stood up and went out into the street, not turning back once. It was dawn. An early baker passed on his motorbike and disappeared around the corner.

From that day, something changed in me. My wife, returning from her business trip, immediately noticed a thoughtfulness that was uncharacteristic in me, but she didn't try to interrogate me. I carried on with my business, but the memory of that night and the girl returned to me constantly.

At the end of the week I told my wife I was going away on business and booked a room in an inexpensive hotel. My wife would not have understood why I was going out after midnight.

This time, when I went out at two a.m., I hoped my feet would take me there intuitively. And so it was. The same hoarding, the same cinema. I put a coin in the slot and the turnstile let me in. The screen was barely lit, but I could just about see the sleeping girl. Leaning in next to her was a bearded man.

This time I had brought some chewing gum and, chewing nervously, I sat in the middle of the empty auditorium and couldn't take my eyes from the screen. The bearded man was snoring and the girl, hugged awkwardly in his arms and legs, was breathing quietly. They turned over a couple of times, facing each other or back-to-back, and at dawn the man woke and, stretching contentedly, tumbled on top of the sleeping girl. Still sleeping, she didn't protest and he, kissing her, did as he wanted.

Then they slept again until six-thirty. At six-thirty the man, naked, headed towards the bathroom, while the girl turned and continued to sleep.

* * *

From that time on, I began to frequent the cinema regularly. Sometimes I went in the daytime, sometimes at night. During the day I would meet other spectators, but if I attempted to speak to them, none would reply. Or they would mumble something and walk away quickly.

I decided to talk to some locals, but they too, when I started asking about the cinema, looked at me as if I were doing something indecent. One elderly woman even spat in my face.

It was odd, but I had stopped thinking about the makers of the film and about the nature of *avant-garde* cinema. Those problems had simply dropped away. I only knew that in that cinema I would always be able to find that familiar girl, who was a stranger to me no more. Most importantly, I knew she was there on the screen living every moment of her life, as I lived mine. That was clear. I began to think about her more frequently. I would disappear for an hour or so from work in the middle of the day and my feet would carry me to the familiar hoarding. I would drop in, sometimes for twenty minutes, sometimes just for one, just to reassure myself that the film hadn't finished, and that the girl still existed. For some reason it had become important to me.

At times I would catch her talking to people who were unfamiliar to me, sometimes with her colleagues, and often to the bearded man. She chatted with her mother regularly on the telephone (and once, finally, I saw her when she came to visit her daughter). For hours on end she would soak in the bath. It all interested me. Who was that man? I would ask myself, seeing him next to her. And I would listen attentively to their endless, lifelike conversation and attempt to work out what it was that kept them together.

Of course, all this was amusing. But not entirely. I understood that the girl was an actress, that the essence of this *avant-garde* creation was that she lived on screen twenty-four hours a day, not two. Like me. I also noticed an ironic note on the cinema hoarding. In the place where they usually wrote the date and time of the film, it said: 'It never ends'.

The note kind of calmed me; it was as if somebody was reassuring me that the girl wouldn't disappear. For some reason I needed to know that. The idea that she was not there anymore, oddly, scared me. She couldn't be the product of my fantasy. She definitely existed, just as that out-of-the-way cinema existed. If needed, it could all be verified immediately.

Having grown used to the auditorium and its smell, I began to pay attention to the other occasional cinema-goers I bumped into from time to time. I had the strange feeling that I had seen them before. Of course, I had seen many of them in the same auditorium, in the same seats. A sullen youngster in a sweater sat in the corner; he had been sat there the previous week too, under a cloud. A plain girl with a sour face always settled in the next to last row. How come I hadn't noticed her before?

Once, having told my wife I was going on a business trip again, I went to stay at a hotel. Upon arriving at the cinema at three a.m. I was surprised to find the plain girl there, pulling continually on her long, curved nose. She bit her plump lips and gazed at the screen. From the lingering twilight of the bedroom, you could hear water dripping in the kitchen.

'Excuse me,' I said in a half-whisper, scaring myself. 'Do you come here often?'

The girl by the wall, lit by the light from the screen, turned nervously towards me.

'Have I scared you?'

She came up to me, wringing her hands.

'I'm terribly unhappy.'

'Why?'

'I'm lonely, I have nobody except . . .' She exhaled. 'Except Liz.'

'Is she a friend?' I asked.

'No, it's her.' The girl pointed at the screen.

'I see.'

'Do you think I'm mad?'

'No.'

'We grew up together, you know.'

'That's impossible.' I was surprised.

'She . . . She . . .' The girl was very agitated. 'I saw her that size. I was nine then.'

'When?' I didn't understand.

'When I saw her the first time.'

'Where? Do you know the actress?'

'Of course, not. I saw her here, on this screen.'

We were standing in the aisle, alone in the half-lit auditorium.

'Wait,' I said. 'Do you mean that the film . . .'

'Yes, it never ends.' The girl sighed with an air of desperateness. 'I was nine the first time I stumbled across this place.'

'I came across it by accident too,' I said, for some reason.

'Everybody comes here by accident. That is by fate. Fate!'

She suddenly frowned sadly and began to weep, not at all embarrassed. I would even say she wept with some satisfaction.

'I'm cursed,' she whispered through her tears.

'No! Why do you say that?' I wanted to console her somehow. 'You seem young and healthy.'

'I'm ugly, can't you see?' She continued to cry, smearing her tears with her fist, like a child.

It felt odd; a total stranger unexpectedly opening her heart and talking about things she probably wouldn't tell anybody. A strange cinema. Strange nights.

'And you, are you happy?' she asked, having stopped crying. 'Why don't you tell me anything about yourself?'

The direction the conversation was taking surprised me a little. On the street I would have thought the tiny scarecrow of a girl was mad. Here, though, other rules reigned; everything was different here. I, myself, was different here.

'Me? What could I tell you about myself? Well, if you're interested: I have a job, a wife, a daughter, probably not much older than you.'

'I asked if you were happy.' She pinned me down, as if she had the right to demand an answer from me. Wasn't that strange?

And that is why, to be honest, I replied, 'Well, you see, my job is quite good, my wife . . . Yes, you're right. Yes, I . . . You know, I think that everything is okay. What else is missing? What else does a man need?'

'A man needs a lot, an awful lot,' the girl said seriously, touching the bridge of her nose with two fingers. 'I'm not sure that I need a man at all. I'm not sure.'

Word of honour, it wasn't easy to follow her train of thought. She showered me with questions, then jumped back to herself. It was difficult.

'What I wanted to say,' she continued, full pelt, while (ridiculously) massaging the sharp tip of her nose, 'was that I had a chance. But, then, why am I alone? Do you understand?'

'No,' I confessed honestly.

Suddenly, she leant towards me on tiptoes and whispered in my ear.

'I like loneliness.'

'But you . . . You're suffering.'

Again, she raised herself on her tiptoes and whispered.

'I like suffering.'

She was clear enough, but it was all quite strange. To be totally honest, I couldn't say that the strangeness didn't please me, or that I wished to get out of there and find myself back in the sunlit street where passers-by constantly scurried about their business.

Ordinary life, which was easy to understand with its decent laws, seemed suddenly banal. I'm not saying it was entirely comfortable, in that poorly-lit auditorium, standing next to the little scarecrow who kept pulling on her already too-long nose. It was far from comfortable. Everything was opaque, strange, and my nerves were as tense as a string. I no longer understood who I was or what, to be honest, I was doing there.

'I want to tell you . . . Are you listening?' The girl pushed herself away. 'I wanted to be pretty, but . . . Here, look.'

She stuck out her hand, right under my nose.

Without a clue what she wanted, I examined her fingers. What was coming next?

'See? The nails! Do you see?'

'I do.'

'They're dirty, can you see. I don't clean under my nails *on purpose*.'

'But why?' I was surprised. 'For goodness sake, what's that all about?'

'I do it because I'm a *scarecrow*. Listen. When I go into a café, I stick out my nails on purpose. And I pull at my nose all the time.'

'Jesus, why?'

'They look at me, all of them, at my nose, do you understand? And so I start pulling at it in front of them. I keep doing it until they turn away.'

'I think you exaggerate the length of your nose.' Once again, I attempted my earlier tactic of trying to pacify her. 'It's all relative: ugly – beautiful. It all depends on a person's temperament, their body language, honesty . . .'

'I know you're unhappy too,' she said, suddenly. 'Here in the cinema, it's empty. The city is sleeping. I couldn't care less now. We could lie down here, in the aisle. Even though my nose is ugly, I'm still a woman. You hadn't forgotten, had you?'

I was speechless.

'But what for? For five minutes of physical pleasure and that's it. It's nothing, do you understand? A flash. It wouldn't solve anything. Nothing.'

'Of course, you're right.' I agreed.

'Thank you.' She grabbed my hand in the darkness and squeezed it. I stood there surprised. It was all so different from ordinary life where everything was clear. She was mad, that was clear. But, on the other hand, you wouldn't get bored with her. I could see something deep in her.

'You know . . .' I began.

'I push dirt under my nails *on purpose* before leaving home,' she whispered into my ear again. 'I could give you my body as a present. It is clean. But I don't want to. Lots of men wanted to marry me, you wouldn't believe it! But it's not what I want.'

Suddenly there was a sound. I had totally forgotten about the film. The screen grew bright.

'It's the doorbell!' The little scarecrow shuddered with excitement. 'It's *him*!'

'Who?'

'You don't know anything about Serge? God, he's going to kill her now! I thought so. I knew. I knew it!'

She left me and ran to her seat. There, pressed against the wall, she fixed her eyes on the screen.

I stood for a while and then went to my row.

'Serioza, is that you?'

The girl on the screen, her naked body dressed in a skimpy dressing gown, stood at the door, face-to-face with an unfamiliar man.

'You didn't expect me?'

'It's late, Serioza. Come tomorrow.'

'Why are you treating me this way? It hurts. Foxie . . .' The man, who was still very young, leaned towards her. 'Tomorrow you'll run away from me again. I know it.'

'I won't run anywhere. I live here.'

'Foxie. Don't you remember me? *My dear sister*. I . . .' His voice trembled.

'Get out! Get out!' She suddenly began to push him out. 'I won't live with you.'

'Why? Have you forgotten everything? You swore, my little Foxie . . .' He resisted, preventing her from closing the door.

'Serioza, try to understand,' she said, in a different tone now. 'I remember everything. I know – you are wonderful, you're going to be big.'

'Did you get my poems?'

'Yes, they're fantastic. But, try to understand, I need some peace in my life. I need calm. A simple life. And with you . . .'

'I'll try, do you hear? Don't push me away . . .'

'No, no!' She shook her head nervously. 'You're not capable of being different, you can't. You know that yourself.'

'Foxie, *I'm your echo*, you do remember, don't you? *I am your echo, your echo in the mountains*. I tried so hard to find you after you disappeared . . . I suffered . . .'

'Don't look for me.' Her voice grew stronger. 'I said, I won't live with you. That's it.'

'But why? Why can't you forgive me for that night? I was beside myself. It wasn't me, was it?'

'Serioza, please don't torture me, leave. I have my own life.'

'Are you married?'

'Yes.'

'You bitch!'

Unexpectedly he swung his fist and hit her in the face. She moaned and fell.

'You're going to get it now, you bitch!'

His face changed. His eyes flashed feverishly. He looked like he was about to do something more but couldn't bring himself to. Shaking, he stood over her prone body for another couple of seconds, then suddenly he turned and ran down the stairs.

The girl lay on the floor with her arms theatrically thrown over her head. A minute later she stood up groaning and, having locked the door, headed towards the bathroom, crying, holding her palm against her cheek.

I tore my eyes from the screen and looked back. The actress switched on the light in the bathroom, illuminating the face of the little scarecrow, who was firmly pressed against the wall. She seemed to be trembling.

From that time, I often saw her there in the cinema at midnight, and sometimes in the daytime. But she, now totally wild, didn't seem to notice me at all.

I also noticed the boy in the sweater. Had he been coming for a long time? Was it possible to come here year after year? I was shaken. Why didn't the newspapers write about this? Why did nobody know about this cinema? And who had created the film? Who was showing it? Even if everything was automated, there still needed to be someone to check and repair the equipment. And to take the money, too. Even though there would not have been much that went into the machine, there must have been somebody to take the money out.

I attempted to talk to the boy in the sweater, and another old man who occasionally sat at the end of the first row. It could not have been by chance that they were there; they must have known something. But it was difficult to find the right moment. I don't know what had made me so brave with the scarecrow. She was a woman and we were alone in the cinema that night. That must have given me the courage. It's silly, of course, but it's always pleasant to see a woman's anxious glance when you address her unexpectedly. You are a man, in control of the situation. It's different then, so much simpler.

How should I address a sullen specimen of my own gender? He wouldn't be worried, quite the opposite: he would probably look me up and down angrily and try to humiliate me. A female stranger can't humiliate you, that's what makes it easy.

And another thing that made my task difficult was that it was impossible to know when any of the men would leave (I couldn't approach them when they were watching the film!) and, as the film had no end, they would come and go whenever they unexpectedly fancied it.

Then one day I had a direct encounter with the boy in the sweater as he was leaving the auditorium.

'Excuse me.' I stopped him as he rushed out. 'Would you mind telling me who the cinema belongs to?'

'I have no idea.' He shrugged his shoulders, unfriendly.

'But are there any ushers?'

I felt silly, but it was not just about the information, now, but more about fulfilling my plan. I had to find out everything, even if he thought me a nuisance.

'How would I know?' the boy mumbled without looking at me, still unfriendly.

'Haven't you ever seen them?'

'Never.'

'And you're not in the least interested who shows the film and what it's all for?'

'Not in the least.'

He kept shuffling his feet nervously, wanting to leave.

'Sorry, but have you been coming here long?'

Suddenly he stopped moving his feet, froze and fixed his gaze upon me, suspiciously. Anger flashed in his eyes.

'What business is it of yours? Who are you?'

Feeling that my question had touched something deep in his heart, I whispered my apology and rushed towards the turnstile.

After that I didn't dare ask anybody else, though once I heard a young couple asking the old man who would sit on the front row, 'Could you tell us when the film starts?'

'The film never ends,' he said and disappeared into the dark auditorium, leaving the couple surprised. I rushed towards him from my position by the turnstile. The conversation started by the couple had given me a kind of pretext to carry on.

'Do you know, by any chance, who the cinema belongs to?'

The elderly gentleman stopped for a second and looked into my eyes with the same distaste as the boy in the sweater had shown. As if I had said something forbidden and indecent.

'*I don't know.*'

I slotted the coin in the turnstile and almost ran inside.

That was my final attempt. I understood that they were not in the least bit interested in anything concerning the showing of the film. For them it was enough that the film and the cinema existed. And that was another strange thing. They looked as if they were afraid to interfere with the domain where the film *was being created*: and that inexplicable fear converted into anger. Or, perhaps, they too were interested in the very things I was. They must have been. They just forbade themselves from sticking their noses where it was prohibited, and, irritatingly, I *kept reminding* them of their secret, their subdued inquisitiveness.

Anyway, I would be no good as a psychoanalyst, so I didn't spend too much time analysing their reactions. At the end of the day, I wouldn't have been particularly pleased if somebody had started quizzing me about how long I had been going there and who was showing the film.

One beautiful day I decided to take a different tack and inspect the other side of the cinema building. There must be a door labelled 'Staff Only'. There must be a staff entrance. There I would bump into whoever was on duty, or a mechanic come to run a daily check of the equipment.

I circled the old, shabby building. There were only two doors on the other side and that was it. They led to the stairwells. Nothing unusual about that; it was often the case that on the first floor you might find offices instead of flats. I inspected both staircases thoroughly, every floor, and even looked in the basements. There were no official signs. Only the numbers of the flats. What a waste of time. It looked like people lived there; there were curtains in the windows and flower pots. But I didn't see a soul. Somebody must live there!

I rang the doorbell on the ground floor determinedly. Nobody answered. Then I rang all the doorbells on the second floor, the third, the fourth . . . I grew more and more agitated as I ran from one flat to another, from one floor to the next. I was desperate to get an answer from somebody living there. Otherwise . . . Otherwise what? I wouldn't have been able to tell you what.

Finally, an old woman answered a door on the second floor.

'Excuse me, could you tell me where the staff door for the cinema is?'

'I don't know,' the woman said, her brow puckered.

'You see,' I lied fervently, 'I have an important parcel for the mechanic. Do you know where he might be?'

'I don't know.'

'And anyway, what type of cinema is it?'

This was, of course, the most ridiculous question. Still, I didn't expect the reaction I got. Without a word, the woman slammed the door in my face.

There are many discourteous people in the world. Some people exist with seemingly no interest in anything. Anyway, why should anybody in the building, who probably didn't even go to the cinema, know where the staff entrance was? Though the entrance had to be somewhere, did it not?

Having calmed down, I decided to check out every floor so I didn't have to come back again. I rang each and every one of the door bells until (a miracle!) another person answered. This time it was a (second miracle!) young and pleasant woman. She, too, had no idea about the cinema.

'There's always somebody coming here to enquire about it,' she told me.

'About what?'

'The same as you. They look for some kind of staff entrance. They have a parcel for the mechanic. Don't be surprised that people get annoyed.'

'No, no. I do understand.'

I was in seventh heaven to be speaking with a normal person. I too, began to feel like a normal person again.

'You know,' the woman in the doorway said, 'all these people are very strange. Nervous somehow. What do they need to find the staff entrance for? They all want to know who the cinema belongs to. How do we know? Honestly, none of us are interested in that cinema.'

'Do you by any chance remember a boy? He is tall, wears sports shoes and a jumper?'

'There have been lots of them. As you probably know, this has been going on for years. When I was still a child they had already started coming asking where the staff entrance is. Where the staff entrance is! It's enough to drive you mad.'

'Did they used to come often?'

'No, not often, but systematically. Once every three to six months, but they definitely came. Most people are at work in the daytime, but I'm at home with the children.'

'So you don't remember a boy in a jumper and sports shoes?'

'Sports shoes?' The woman was thinking. 'Yes, I remember now! Did the jumper have a deer knitted on the chest?'

'Yes. So he did come here?' I was overjoyed.

'The year before last he . . .' The woman laughed.

'What?'

'He fell over, down there.' She indicated a small step behind me. 'He was so nervous, he fell over as he ran downstairs. I saw because my door was still open. He smashed his nose; I took him to my bathroom to wash his face. Then he lay on our sofa with a compress until it stopped bleeding. He kept asking whose cinema it was.'

'So you really don't know?'

'How would I know? Why do you all need to know? I don't understand.'

It occurred to me that she had suddenly realised that she was talking too much and looked at me suspiciously for the first time.

'You must agree,' I said, 'that there should be a staff entrance to the cinema.'

'Probably . . .' She sighed.

'But . . . *It's not there.*' I spoke so passionately that her eyes grew suspicious again.

'If it's not there, then it isn't there; why are you so worried about it?'

'How can it be though? How can a cinema not have a staff entrance?'

'But why are you so concerned?' she repeated, as sincerely surprised as I was. But she still (good girl!) forced a smile.

‘It’s not right, a cinema without a staff entrance!’

‘And what *business* is it of yours?’

‘But . . .’ I was astonished by her logic. ‘For goodness sake, is it possible?’

‘Is this really the biggest problem in your life?’ She was still smiling, though she seemed a touch annoyed.

‘No, but I still can’t understand . . .’

‘I’m sorry . . . My children.’ She forced a reticent smile and, without waiting for my reply, stepped back, closing the door in front of me.

I felt an utter fool. At least she had heroically forced a smile. So there were people who knew how to be polite, who knew how to communicate with madmen like me. It was awful; what on earth had I been going on about? Obviously, she thought I was mad.

I ran downstairs, my glance again skimming the doors. No, there were just the numbers to the flats.

My head spun slightly. So it was clear that somebody else had been trying to find out who it was showing the film, trying to solve the mystery. Great. And it was clear that he had learned nothing. Then what had happened to him over the years? Why did he stop looking for the truth? Was he pleased that the film didn’t end (it was unclear why and how, but, still, it *did not end*) and that at any time, on the slightest whim, you could come, put a coin in the slot and enter into the world of that character, who aged exactly as you did?

Those *avant-gardistes* came up with some pretty weird stuff. I attempted to reassure myself and calm myself down. But I was different from those oddballs, they were a different story. It could all be very simple and carefully planned, with no supernatural explanation. They could have just put a flat number on the staff entrance, as if it was a private apartment. What a great idea! To separate yourself from the audience by a Wall of China, to not allow them, mesmerised by the film, to enter the divine area where they were creating something endless. Modernism!

I felt that I had made a step forward; I had revealed a secret. A simple puzzle. It could be that a whole corporation was looking after this small suburban cinema. Why not? It could be that a whole *cinematic enterprise* was hiding behind this shroud of total, absolute secrecy. It was, after all, no joke to create a film over such a *long* period of time, even if nothing particular happened in it. Though at the end of the day, it might not be so difficult to achieve: you sign a contract with the mother of a small girl for a period of her life. Say for the first ten years. And as the girl grows, you film her, yes? Though not twenty-four hours a day. Why would you? Contemporary technology, with its potential for montage, loops . . . It would be enough to film her for half an hour, then you could make eight hours and repeat it for the whole year, with some variations. When it comes down to it, most things that we do, we do *day in day out*, the same again and again. Ninety per cent of our time is spent in routine activities; cleaning our teeth the same way every day; frying an omelette the same way. It all repeats and there is little occasion for surprises. You could film all the 'events' of the year in a month. So it could be that the little girl only worked for one month a year, but was paid by some corporation for a year. And the next year, a bit older now, they filmed her for another month.

Fine. I was impressed by my intellectual abilities. It all added up. Ten years on, the girl wouldn't disappear; she would have got used to living at the expense of the film studio. Now it would be her, not her mother, who signed the contract for another ten years. Or possibly for the rest of her life.

So, you drop into a tiny suburban cinema and have no idea that behind all this *weirdness* (shrouded in anonymity) hides a cinematographic corporation and exact calculations.

There was just one thing that wasn't clear: what was it all for? Money? A psychological experiment?

The thought that I was little more than a guinea pig in a trap made me feel sick. And the money – there would not be much of it, despite the regular clients. But what did I know? perhaps there were self-service cinemas scattered all over the country, or worldwide. Maybe, when you added up the coins from the thousands of these kinds of cinemas frequented by poor oddballs, they combined into a powerful, rushing stream of money, and there was somebody standing there under the stream with a sack, chuckling contentedly as they raked in the money.

Meanwhile, time passed and these unhealthy thoughts (how else would you characterize them?) vanished. I simply grew tired of them. What did I get out of them, those thoughts? I thought I understood the cinema-going oddballs a little better now; they didn't bother about trifles and came simply for the sake of coming. My head hurt from thinking; it all seemed terribly complicated. Also, I wasn't entirely sure it wasn't just the result of my over-active imagination. Actually, it *was* the fruit of my imagination – what else? I had no facts. All that stuff about a powerful film company, the atmosphere of secrecy, the contract with the little girl's mother – I had simply *invented* that. Which, in fact, had been a pointless exercise. I had probably just *failed to find* the door labelled 'Staff only'. I had just missed it. It was hidden somewhere in an out-of-the-way corner. If I had found it (I hadn't been back to look) and had opened the door, I would have discovered a very old mechanic working at the projector, who would have explained everything simply and fully, for example that the automatic cashier is profitable as it is cheaper than employing someone, and the film is delivered from a studio that usually makes feature films but occasionally, from their profits, funds *avant-garde* projects like this one. And for him and his son, the owners, it's profitable to show such films, as regular audiences emerge who keep visiting for decades, and it's more important to get a guaranteed income, even if it isn't huge, rather than take risks and depend on chance. Also, the old man would go on, sometimes people come at night, too, (when have you ever seen that?) and put money in the machine. It makes enough to cover the basics. And as far as the title *It Never Ends* is concerned, that was my nephew, Georgie, who came up with it, he's such a joker . . .

This version was pure fantasy too. My head was splitting from all these ideas, these suppositions, but it was only then – I repeat, only then – that I started to understand the other uncommunicative, odd visitors.

Having chased away any thought of *how?* and *when?* I was once more alone in front of the screen. After three months of intensive speculation, one night at midnight I entered the completely empty cinema auditorium as if for the first time. I sat in the middle row. For a while the sense of annoyance lingered; I was still disturbed by the thoughts I had had for such a long time.

As always, the girl on the screen was sleeping peacefully. As always, the alarm clock ticked. Water dripped in the kitchen.

I sat with my head sunk between my shoulders, attempting to resurrect my former feelings. What on earth had made me attempt to find out who and why? Was it so bad to not know anything? My stupid analytical brain had ruined the miracle. It would have been better to have remained ignorant. And, anyway, what had I learned? Nothing.

For some time, I struggled to relate to what was going on the screen. But as the minutes passed, the total silence and the darkness of the cinema auditorium entered into me. The city was sleeping, as was the girl on the screen. I sat absolutely alone in that city, in that cinema, lit by the screen.

My life returned to its normal course. I still tried to work out what was going on: I called various cinematic organisations, and the Ministry of Culture, but nothing. No result. What was most interesting, was that nobody had ever heard of the cinema! I decided, for the time being, not to call the tax inspectors to set their dogs on the cinema, forcing them to explain to the financial experts how it was all possible: a small cinema in the suburbs of the capital city, that was not on anybody's records. It looked incredibly suspicious and difficult to explain. The cinema must exist in the central tax records, from which you couldn't hide a needle in a haystack.

This time, though, I felt once more the half-forgotten pleasant wave of warmth flood over me. Once again, I was plunged into something strange and mysterious, which I had no desire to try to understand. And the more I avoided trying to understand, the more the idea of a *cinematic corporation* and *elderly owner* seemed ridiculous. No, there were *some things you could not explain* in essence. Some things were a mystery.

It felt as if there was, in fact, no such cinema – and yet it was there! Wasn't that its peculiar charm? What would happen if I led the government tax inspectors there by hand? They would include the little cinema in their statistics and start working out how the film was rented, was it twenty-four hours a day?

Most importantly, I was not completely sure that what I would find with the government officials would be the same as what I found myself when I visited on my own at midnight. It was a strange and yet, at the same time, quite a realistic feeling. I couldn't tell *what* I expected to find there instead: a fishmonger's, or an ordinary cinema showing two-hour films? In short, I was not entirely convinced that this institution was real. Which was stupid, if you thought about it. But I'm talking here about my feelings, not about whether the cinema really existed and that I occasionally went there, putting a real coin into the slot of the machine.

And so the first year passed. My daughter had returned from the sanatorium, but she brought back with her a lanky boy with a plait and glasses.

'Meet my husband.'

This was like a bucket of cold water on my head. And seven months later a tiny wrinkled face. 'U-a! u-a! u-a!'

It was no good trying to resist it, of course, as it was only to be expected, but my wife and I were not prepared, and that was the problem! That was what annoyed me. A granddaughter, falling on our heads so unexpectedly, didn't make us happy. To be honest, I was not really sure what had happened. It was all too unexpected. I remembered, then, my own mother once being so against me rushing into marriage: now I knew exactly what she had meant! If I had longed for a son-in-law, a grandchild, it would have been different; I would have been brimming with joy. At last! Finally! A son-in-law and a grandchild.

Unfortunately, it had struck neither my wife nor I, when we had accompanied our Niurochka to the sanatorium, that she was ready to become a mother and so on. Theoretically we could have foreseen it, of course, but not *now*! Not at that moment. And who was he, this Valik with a plait? Where had she found him? (So it was because of him that she had stayed there for so long!)

In short, my daughter had a hysterical fit and my wife fainted. Then there was a premature birth etc. Valik, with his plait, scowled at us and said, 'Don't worry, we'll rent a flat.' In other words, we are capable of looking after ourselves. For my daughter I became nothing more than a vacant space, way below Valik in importance. I had been an empty space before, but now that she had Valik her father sounded indifferent and cold. Short-tempered. My daughter didn't love me. Not at all.

My wife blamed me for everything; it was I who had spoiled her. I had allowed her to go to late-night films. As if she wouldn't have found Valik without those late-night films.

'It was you. You decided to send her to that sanatorium!'

'Will you stop! Don't blame me.'

It was all so sad. We had once been so close, my wife and I and our baby, when she had been our little fair-haired girl. The dawn of our lives. We were full of bright dreams. What was left?

A year had passed from the time I had first stumbled across the cinema. It existed for me, though it was non-existent itself. Having been drawn into the whirlpool of problems that had descended upon me (I had also been demoted at work), I kept forgetting everything. I felt like I was boiling in a pot, experiencing little pleasure, but a growing despair. My God! At home my wife was all business-like, moaning constantly; at work – demotion; my daughter had found this Valik and escaped with him to an apartment of their own. Oh my Lord! What was all this? Why? There were financial difficulties and all kinds of other stuff. Lord! Was this really me?

When I closed my eyes my youth would play out before my eyes; there were mountains, seas, mighty foaming waves. And me, by myself in the cool of the pink foaming elements (the sun was setting). The waves licking my feet. I was still nobody; young, talented, with no knowledge of life. I was sincere. I was nobody and *everybody*.

Over the years I had grown cunning and cynical (but what had I achieved? Had I achieved anything *special*?) I shouted at my wife when she exhausted me with her silliness, and *I was very close* to hating my daughter, who, with her posturing, kept trying to prove that she was independent, that she had Valik. And when I put her in her place, she grew afraid of me. Afraid and full of hate. And myself? I would have given anything to be united with her again, the way we had been not so long before, a happy father and daughter.

Unfortunately, everybody thought of me as an egotist, being egotists themselves. That was how it was; how else could you characterize it? But why? It was not true. I still had *something* in me. Why did nobody see it? Why?

The cinema. I began to go more frequently. When I decided to go on a *business trip*, everything suddenly became so much simpler. I would be able to turn a blind eye to what had annoyed me the day before. I would smile faintly to my wife's refrain: 'Volodia, your jacket! You just throw it anywhere.' In my head, I was already packing my travel bag.

'Volodia, Nura's breasts are painfully inflamed. Volodia, are you listening? We need to go around to see her, she called,' my wife said.

'Can't you see, I'm going on a business trip,' I replied with a smile. 'Send her my love.' And in my head I would add, 'Be happy, my Nura.'

In those moments I felt good. Why? Because I also had (wasn't it strange) something that was mine. My daughter had Valik; she clung to him tightly. My wife had a job and her daughter (they were brought closer together by female secrets and interests). And me? My job meant nothing anymore; it was just a job, a gloomy place to hang about, a waiting that lasted eight hours a day (still three hours left, one more hour . . .). No, it so happened, that I was left with one thing that I could call *mine*.

Which was, of course, my cinema. If a year before somebody had suggested such a thing, I would have laughed heartily. I wouldn't have believed that some strange little cinema, some nocturnal activities, some film could turn into such a powerful habit. What else was there, if not this?

Sadly, I had nobody to hold on to. If I had had a son instead of a daughter, maybe everything would have turned out differently. We would have had something of our own, a man's thing. But I had a daughter instead, with inflamed breasts; all her secrets were a woman's secrets and they belonged to my wife only. Why was it so?

I understood, though, that it wasn't just an injustice, it was the highest type of injustice, which you just have to accept. Such was life. But how was I to live? Life bubbled, erupted with problems, hysterical feelings, chores; it was all so monotonous. From morning till night I had to listen to: 'Nurochka needs', 'Nurochka said', 'Nurochka asked.' Obviously, I understood that everything centred around a baby's birth. I knew what it meant to be a young mother. My daughter! It couldn't have been any other way, could it?

Even earlier in my life, home hadn't been the centre of my life. Still, there had been some slight hint of it – my family, my wife, my daughter, me. There was something which, though not too tightly bound, was integral. It was a triangle. One way or another, there was my family. Recently, though, I had begun to experience an anxious feeling of fragility, a weakening of the ties for some unknown reason. But my family still was there.

And then it fell apart. Valik with his plait appeared, as if he had dropped from the sky. I still jumped when I heard, 'My baby, come to your daddy, come.' *Daddy* wasn't me, it was this Valik slobbering over *his* daughter, scowling at me. Who was I to him? *Who* was this stranger to me? And their (*their*) baby?

Now my wife would disappear to the other flat, which my daughter had rented with her chosen one. Quite quickly they were getting on: I noticed that Valik smiled at my wife, even if wryly. And why not? It hadn't taken her long to overcome the shock. She drew herself into the cycle of everyday chores, taking on the most onerous jobs. She washed, she cooked meals, she fussed about the consultations, she arranged the doctor's home visits, she tidied the flat. Quite simply, she surprised me; some instinct had budded in her, a passion, there was no other way to describe it. No other way to describe that activity that lit up in her. How quickly she had been able to get over the shock! Each day she felt more and more like a grandmother, even if a *young* one. And, in her own way, she was proud of that.

So she got over the shock with a bustle that arose from passion alone. But where was *I* to get that passion from? I looked inside myself and wasn't able to find it. There was nothing, apart from an increasing emptiness and loneliness.

My daughter, my wife and that Valik had all entered a new phase in their lives, a new stage. They failed to notice that I had been left behind. Every day, every week, I fell further and further away from them, the pace accelerating. Finally, I realised that they had grown very far from me, so terribly far, and that I, having been left in the past, would never be able to catch up with them.

Was that my egotism? Yes, but I didn't want to feel that way. I envied my wife, my daughter and her young and confident Valik; they were all so passionate and excited. They lived for some exciting future. I realised I couldn't experience the feelings that excited them and drew them close together. I couldn't. I wished I could, but I was not able. They weren't there in me. Had I grown old? It was true that it felt to me that my life was over.

The closer they became, bound by mutual chores, the more that feeling grew in me. That feeling of alienation. But what could I do? Being a man, how could I get closer to them? Wash the nappies? Cook dinner for Valik? I would drop in on them occasionally and would be confronted with the miserable face of the lanky guy with a plait. 'What do you, you old wreck, need with my family?' I was convinced he wanted to say just that. Or so I thought. But, to be honest, what had I done wrong? It was true that I had been against my daughter's wedding because I had been so shocked; I had hoped I could get her to think straight, to persuade her not to rush into things. That was silly. I didn't want *to lose* my daughter so soon. But my wife had been even more hysterical (and she had *egged me on*). My wife, whom Valik now not only tolerated but, I was convinced, also valued more and more.

Justice. I had no right to demand that if I didn't love anybody. But I so wanted to love. I did.

Every time I dropped in, my daughter would glance nervously at her now-lawful husband.

'Come in,' she would say, trying to hide an irritation that I did not understand.

Her plaited husband would appear from the room, but wouldn't say more than, 'Hello', 'Goodbye' (thanks for that anyway). My daughter would take me to the kitchen and pour me some soup that my wife had made. It was an idiotic situation; it looked as if I had come for some food, like some kind of parasite. What else then? It seemed that neither I nor my daughter (who had *left her* daughter for just a short minute) could understand.

In the long run I realised that my daughter was irritated by a feeling of guilt she could not understand, whenever she saw me. And that was not love, rather the contrary; it was an oppressive annoyance.

Once, my daughter opened up, and having brushed the oppressive mood from her face, said, 'Dad, maybe we could talk like two adults now. You behave like I'm a little puppy. You blame me for having got married against your wishes. I can feel it. But you don't want to understand, you don't even try to understand that I am not you, I am a different person with my own fate, Dad. You have lived a long life with my mum, you've had your happiness and worries. So why don't you want me to have mine? You don't like Valik. Dad, I have a husband, a child; I am in no way worse than you. I am the same as you, a grown-up. I have my own family. I am an adult.'

The only thing she left out, if you thought about it logically was, 'I am an adult. *I am not your daughter*.'

I said nothing. I muttered something and left, smiling quietly. That probably annoyed her even more as she clearly didn't understand my smile; it was the only way I could shield myself from her arrows. There was one thing I knew for sure, those words were not my daughter's. That was not my daughter, but an annoyed lady of leisure, who had been forced to retreat from her husband, from *her* baby, for a second, in order to pour out everything she thought about me. It simply was not my daughter speaking, it was clear. I felt better immediately, the moment I understood this. No, my daughter . . . She loved me.

So I smiled quietly on my way out.

I half-ran in the direction of the cinema; I fell over twice. It was dark, and I kept stumbling over the kerbs as I crossed the streets. The idea that the cinema might be closed made my blood run cold. Of course, I knew it couldn't be the case, but fear kept me tight. *What* would I do all night if the cinema was closed? I couldn't imagine anything more terrifying.

It was open, that little cinema of mine, so quiet, so forgotten by everybody, so cosy. It was the only one open, with its light flickering in the middle of the dead, concrete, sleeping city.

When I went in, the little scarecrow was sat in her usual place, on her own in the empty auditorium. She watched as Liz slept. Yes, Liz.

I hurried over to the scarecrow, who was pulling at her long nose. Strangely, she didn't seem at all surprised. She stood up and looked at me, waiting.

'Oh my God,' I said losing any sense of perspective. 'You can't imagine how bad I feel.'

'Calm down,' the scarecrow said and with unexpected boldness pulled me towards herself and put my head upon her chest. 'Calm down.'

I could not hold myself back and began to cry.

'I know you feel bad, I do,' said the scarecrow. 'You poor thing.'

'I didn't want,' I said, wiping my tears. 'I didn't want that.'

'I know.'

'I . . . So, it seems that nobody needs me.'

'I knew you were lonely. I knew.' She was stroking my hair. 'I would like to give you my body as a present.'

'No. What for?' I was sobbing.

'Poor you,' the scarecrow went on. 'Nobody loves you.'

'How do you know?'

'I can feel it.'

'I . . .'

'Let's lie here, on the floor.' She was caressing my shoulders. 'Please calm down, sweetheart. My baby. I will save you.'

Where did she find those words? How did she know what words I needed to hear and in what kind of a voice?

'I . . . I'm old,' I said to her. 'I'm old and you are young. You are like my daughter.'

'And so what?' she whispered in my ear. 'You are suffering. I . . . I will be your daughter.'

'My daughter?'

'Yes. I am your daughter. Can't you feel it? I'm ready to give you everything.'

I knew. I knew it. My daughter – she loved me.

'But how?' I said. 'You . . . Me . . . It's a cinema.'

'Simple,' the scarecrow whispered. 'I will touch you, that's all. You'll get excited. You will definitely get excited. And then . . .'

'No,' I whispered.

'Yes, yes. I want it. You're suffering.'

In that moment we both were truly mad, because a person in their right mind wouldn't be able to feel so close to a stranger, wouldn't feel about them the way a wife could or a daughter. It was all totally incomprehensible. Especially when, in the half-light (Liz's bedroom was illuminated on the screen), I took the scarecrow to be my daughter. And it happened only because she uttered the words (how did she know?) and in the intonation which I had been waiting to hear from my daughter all my life. No, I don't mean the scarecrow's suggestion, but rather some mad pity. I was surprised. I had always considered myself to be strong, not needing anybody's pity. A real man. And suddenly, for no apparent reason, I was terribly, insanely in need of that pity.

We lay on the floor, cheek to cheek, while on the screen Liz slept. There was the familiar sound of the alarm clock ticking away. And, as always, water dripped in the kitchen sink.

It was like a dream. Why at night? Why in the cinema? My daughter. I couldn't care less about the physical pleasure, that wasn't important. For the first time in many years I felt so light. That was what was important. For the first time. Without any clear reason. My daughter stroked my hair.

'I will never leave you, never. You are my dearest.' That was truth. She was my daughter. Or somebody else? She loved me.

What was she talking about, that scarecrow? 'Do you think I forgot the past? Forgot who you were to me? Do you think that current life had drowned out everything?' Yes, that was what I was thinking.

We lay on the hard floor and someone sweet, whose naked shoulder I clung to, stroked me as I sobbed.

'Poor, poor you.'

Somebody whispered those words. Somebody felt sorry for me.

Relief came in a sort of convulsive way, while I sobbed, a harmless old man. And the scarecrow held me in her slim arms like a broken but still living doll. I felt ashamed, but she encouraged me and enticed me, enticed me. For what? Until it happened. And then I felt incredibly light, as if somebody had cut the Gordian knot that tied me.

Now I had not only the cinema. And though I didn't want to, I was growing more distant from my wife and my daughter. I held on to them with all my strength. It hurt so much. But now, as if I had crossed a line, everything became clear. I was no longer with them; their alienation did not hurt any more. What had I done?

I had never been unfaithful to my wife, never. And now I had. It was fate then. Of course, it was fate. Had I been aware of what I was doing? Did I feel I was myself? What was slowly pushing me off the track?

My daughter. She was distant now and sweet in her own way. I understood, finally, who she was and who I was. She had her own life, her own fate. She was right. My wife had her own life, too. I was already very far away, on the other side, and from that position, finally, it was easy for me to see how they had their *own* lives. I had no doubt that the scarecrow had helped me to take that fatal step; somehow she had understood that I needed to be dragged to the other side.

'I'm going to the bathroom,' she whispered in my ear. 'Put your trousers on, the floor is cold.'

I managed to dress somehow and sat on an aisle seat. The girl on the screen slept on in the half-light. Occasionally the bedroom was lit by the fleeting light of a passing taxi.

'My dear.'

The scarecrow hurried up to me, happy and excited. She knelt down.

'You . . .' I said.

'Everything is fine. I did what I could.'

She was happy, I could see that.

I stroked her head. She smiled. For a moment her long, bent nose looked so sweet.

'I'm happy,' she said, revealing her feelings at that moment.

'I'm ashamed.' I said how I felt.

'It's nothing. It's better than earlier.'

'Of course,' I whispered.

'Now everything will look simpler.'

'Yes,' I replied. 'And who am I to you?'

'You?' She laughed again (she hadn't used to laugh like that). 'You are everything. Everything.'

'Really?'

'Really. Like Liz.' She pointed at the screen.

'And she is who?' I asked.

'Don't you know? The day before yesterday she took her child to hospital, poor thing.'

'What child?'

'So you don't know anything!' The scarecrow laughed. 'She split up with her husband. And the child . . . And the child . . . She went to see Serioza, she couldn't resist, but she . . . She doesn't want to live with him. She simply can't. Haven't you seen it?'

'No.' I shook my head. 'Recently I've only been coming at night, when she's asleep. I only see how she sleeps.'

'Me too, I really like to watch her sleep.' And looking into my eyes, she ran her finger along her long nose, slightly pulling at its tip. I nearly laughed.

'Oh, you're funny,' I said.

'Yes, you don't really know me.'

'So how could you guess what my life was like?'

'I just felt it. I have no idea how.'

'You spoke the way only my daughter could speak.'

'I could simply feel you. I felt that you needed a daughter. A daughter who . . . Somebody was speaking through me. Oh, look, she's woken up again. She wakes up again and again; she keeps thinking about her child.'

The girl on the screen sat up, rubbing her forehead. The silence rang in our ears.

'She's going to the bathroom, she's going to wash her face,' the scarecrow whispered. 'Do you love her?'

'Yes,' I said. 'I've known her for a year.'

'And I've known her since I was nine. I was still a child. We grew up together. I live her life.'

'And your life?'

'My life?' She looked surprised, as if she was not sure she understood the meaning of my words. 'I don't know. I love Liz.'

I had, of course, committed an act of abuse; I had used the broken mind of a psychiatric patient, a crazy person. Though, who had I used? It was she who led me on all this time, as if I was a child. For some reason she *needed* that; it was obvious. Otherwise she wouldn't have offered herself.

But there, in the cinema, I didn't think of her as not being normal. In the cinema, where the film never ended, one's understanding of normal changed. She was simply a nice, compassionate girl. And her eyes shone with happiness as my burden, that weight that had held me down for so many months, miraculously vanished. I saw that the consequence of my action (if you could call it that) left no residue on her; on the contrary, she shone with pure happiness and vitality. And she opened up to me, as she had ten minutes before: no, even more so. Yes, so that I should feel calm and good with her. It was strange, though; she didn't know me, or my problems and my life, but in those depths where I was all alone, she understood me better than anybody else. I realised then that the ability to feel is no less a gift than the ability to think. She entered into me, having recognised my inner state, without asking about anything. While I had always thought that at difficult moments you needed to talk, to explain, and then to talk again, she surprised me by not trying to delve deeply into what I considered such important detail. She *didn't want to know me* – which seemed strange! But then I realised the value of my concreteness. She approached me with her eyes closed, like a mole underground.

* * *

A year later, I moved in with her. Apart from the shock to my wife and my daughter, everything went smoothly. I don't think my disappearance from their lives was particularly painful. They didn't understand how I could, as they put it, 'betray' them. I, though, couldn't imagine how I could carry on living without some kind of support, so I left when I found one, not because I wanted a good life.

'Dad, how can you? Have you gone mad?' my daughter said, cradling her one-year-old in her arms, saliva all over her face, her empty expression set on me. 'You've got grey hair! I'm ashamed of you, *ashamed*! What will people say?'

I carried on smiling, as I had that time when I left after our first 'open' discussion. That was not my daughter.

'You have a granddaughter, Dad. And you hunt after a skirt my age? What a shame! Shush, shush, baby, don't cry. If you needed that skirt so much, if you don't give a damn for me, or for mum, you could have at least done it in *secret*, couldn't you?'

I kept smiling, sure of one thing: this was *not my* daughter.

'Ha, I can see now! Shush, baby, shush . . . Valik! Valik! Come here. Take Taniusha. Can you hear? Take Taniusha from me, she's howling! Now I can see who you are. You're cynical, Dad. You don't give a toss about any of us. You stand there mocking our words with your cynicism.'

At that my lips trembled slightly. I left hastily, without saying a word. No, that was *not my* daughter.

My daughter loved me.

She was waiting for me in a small flat near the cinema.

'Oh, my poor thing.'

She comforted me as I cried.

'Don't go to them anymore, are you listening? They will insult you every time.'

'Why? Why?' I sobbed.

'*I* was born out of you, do you hear? I am your daughter.'

'Yes.'

I lay in her lap, and she was sorry for me with her wild pity.

I kept hoping that after some months, after some years, we would start to miss each other, recalling our happy past; perhaps it hadn't been wonderful, but it was ours. They would find me. They would come to me having forgiven everything, they would understand that I had loved them too much to accept that they had their own lives.

Unfortunately, they didn't come. And I never had a chance to utter the words I had prepared. 'No, really, I don't deserve praise. I'm the guilty one. Yes, I'm so happy that I can come back to you all and live as I used to. And you who were there for me in my hour of need, forgive me, my life calls me back again. If the path of my life should once more turn away, I will come back to the cinema and look for you, but if not, then forgive me. I'm sorry and good bye.'

Not only did the passing of the years not draw us closer, but, rather, it established the distance between me and my former (now most definitely former) family once and for all.

I bumped into my wife accidentally once, as she was rushing somewhere with a shopping bag. She stopped for a second as if she had noticed a cockroach.

'Ah, it's you, you old womaniser. Not a total drunkard yet?' she said spitefully, her voice hoarse.

Who did they imagine I was? *What* did they think I was?

I didn't have the strength to tear down the barriers. At nights I would cry, unable to stand their insults. I wanted love, I wanted to live with them – with them all.

'Poor you, my poor thing.' The crazy scarecrow, whom I had grown used to considering my daughter, stroked my hair.

But she was only my daughter when I was able to deceive myself. Only then. Only then was I happy to say, 'Here she is, my daughter. She hasn't left me. She loves me.'

Liz lived on her own too, with Serge's baby. The baby of her first love, whom she now hated. Something had urged her to sleep with him that night, so that later, even after the divorce from her husband, she would never have to be close to him again.

We often visited her together. We had no children. The little scarecrow, it turned out, was not able to have any. And anyway, why would we want them?

Our day was split up into three parts. In the mornings we talked about Liz, about what would happen to her that day; then I would help the scarecrow get ready and I would go to work. That was the first part. Then, after work, *we would go to see Liz*. We had long before stopped saying we were going 'to the cinema' or 'to see a film'. Phrases like that came, over the years, to seem more and more blasphemous. It was like saying about your sister or mother, 'her battery went flat'. I would be annoyed at anybody who might ask, 'What film is on?' or, 'Who is this actress?' At times I felt like I might kill somebody for daring to remind me of the words 'film', 'cinema', or 'actress'. For some reason I grew more and more afraid of them; why those innocent words provoked horror and disgust in me, I didn't quite understand.

No longer was there 'cinema', 'film' and 'show' (there were no individual 'shows' anyway). There was just *Liz.* The *Liz* we loved.

We were afraid of everything related to the word 'cinema'. We never went to the cinema. Never. It would have been impossible to enter a *cinema* and watch a *film*: to see, instead of Liz, some actors, the product of somebody's imagination, creativity! As if Liz was somebody's invention! It would have been like going up to your mother and seeing a cable connecting her to the electricity. No. We didn't buy newspapers, so that we wouldn't come across cinema listings accidentally. Most of all, we were afraid of the magazines and books in which they *wrote* about cinema. That was . . . That was equivalent to reading that some clever men had assembled your mother from pieces of scrap metal. No, that would have been unbearable for us.

After going to see Liz, the third part of our day would begin: conversation about what we had seen that day. We would relive it all once more. As we went to bed we saw Liz before us: her eyes, her soul.

How was it possible to live like that? It seemed we could. Never before could I have imagined that I might be able to. Household chores, which I had never really thought about before, became my favourite activity. I looked after the scarecrow, though I was unsure why. It was a pleasure. Her devotion to Liz made her seem spiritual in my eyes. In my mind I associated her with Liz and perceived her through Liz. Liz – her fate was what united our souls.

Bit by bit, I began to enjoy this aimless life. It had been a long time since I had experienced it, though I had longed for it. I had suffered. Now, first thing in the morning, after waking up, I would wash the dishes. What for? Where was the meaning in it? I didn't rack my brain thinking about it! I didn't rack my brain at all. I simply did it, without thinking. Then I would go to the shops and on to work, so that I could bring in some money with which I could go to the shops. Simply for that reason. The scarecrow cooked me dinner and I vacuumed the floor. I vacuumed every day. And cleaned under the cupboards with a wet cloth. What for? Everyday chores bore no relation to life and didn't require the question 'What for?' Unawares, little by little, family life had become life itself. I dived into it as a fish dives into the depths after being tortured on the shore. For six months I painstakingly constructed a small cabinet for the bathroom. It was going to be a *good* cabinet, *skilfully* made, without gaps or rough edges. With ten drawers.

What bliss it was to not have to glance back into the past, to not have a future.

We visited the late-night shows only once a month. It was a special event and we would feel slightly uncomfortable. At night Liz was different to the person we knew in the daytime, when there were other people around. She would often have fits of hysteria at night. It wasn't nice to watch her then, we felt. So we went not more than once a month, which was just about what our conscience allowed us.

Liz would usually sleep through until morning, like people do, and we would sit and watch her quietly. In the daytime we sat together, but once a month, at night, we would sit separately like we used to, each in our own place, I in the middle of the auditorium, the scarecrow by the wall, the row before last. And then I would feel some anxiety: I would suddenly *remember* who I was, where I was. And during that nocturnal hour it appeared to me that I used to have a family. Not the scarecrow, who seemed like something from a nightmare, but *a real family*. A real daughter, a real wife. *I was just like everybody else*. An unfamiliar anxiety would begin to sting my heart and I felt like running out of there (I cast malicious glances at the scarecrow), *I felt* I had a daughter, a *real* daughter, she existed, she lived in the same city and had *her own* daughter, *my granddaughter*; a real granddaughter.

I would weep quietly, unnoticed (the scarecrow was sat behind me), and for the first time in a long while, nobody would feel any compassion for me. But I didn't need anybody's compassion. At such moments I didn't want the scarecrow's pity. I didn't want her to feel sorry for me with her *mad* pity. No, those tears were mine. Only mine.

In the morning, when Liz awoke, and we left the cinema and headed home to sleep (we would always keep that day free), I would forget everything, as if somebody had taken a wet cloth and wiped it from my memory. Until the next night. A month later.

* * *

How long could it go on? For all eternity. Because we had everything. We had *a reason* to live. It was strange that there, in my other, past life, I had so much of everything, but I didn't have a reason to live. I've no idea why. In this new life, you could say that I had nothing, but I had a reason to live: the cabinet, the scarecrow, Liz. Now I lived for *everything*.

So who, actually, was she to me? I had never considered the scarecrow to be my wife. That would have been ridiculous. She could have been my daughter. I was even less inclined to consider her to be my lover; that would have been total nonsense. The scarecrow couldn't be that; she just felt sorry for me. She had given me her body only after having tried everything else; it was the last resort. When I wasn't suffering, we never ever thought about it. I knew for sure that if I had asked her for some kind of pleasure, she wouldn't have let me close to her, and I, too, would have been ashamed.

At times she was like a little dog to me, small and ugly. This was most probably how I considered her. Otherwise why would I have cooked for her, washed her clothes? I didn't feel any of the symptoms of love that a man feels for a woman that they usually describe in books. Who actually loves like that? She wasn't a woman. She was simply a *living being*, a living being in my flat (though, in fact, the flat really belonged to her, even if it seemed the other way around to me). She was like a domestic dog or cat. That's how I thought about her. Actually, from the time I went to live there, I had been living on my own. That was how it was. On my own. The scarecrow was a domestic animal, which I happily fed and bathed and at times rubbed under her ear so that she purred. That was how our life went. It was difficult, anyway, to think of her as human, that scarecrow; she was too strange, too unusual to be a human.

But she wasn't just a random animal who happened to live in the same room as me. She had *saved* me when times were tough. That's the type of animal she was.

At times, when we couldn't go together, we would visit Liz in turns. On one of these occasions the scarecrow didn't seem herself when she ran home. Before I got a chance to ask what had happened, she cowered trembling in the corner by the bed.

'What happened?'

She didn't reply, her eyes gazing blindly.

'What is it?'

'He . . . e . . .' She was short of breath.

'Just say it!'

'He died, this morning.'

I understood without her having to explain. Liz's son had died. He had been ill for the past couple of months. Like Liz, the scarecrow and I had barely slept during those two months. We dropped in to see Liz and suffered with her.

'What can we do?'

'How can she, the poor thing . . .' The scarecrow held on to her long nose and sat like that, as if by doing so she hoped to hide herself from the events that had taken place.

'But why?' I went closer to her. 'He was better yesterday.'

'Yes, but in the night he had a fit again. And . . .'

'And Liz?' I asked.

'She's all by herself, can't you see? She's all alone.'

'And us?' I said.

She looked at me.

'She is all by herself.'

The scarecrow fell on her pillow and lay there, worried.

'Let's go to her,' I said.

'Let's go,' she whispered, and tears streamed down her face.

We both knew that Liz lived on the screen, but she had become so much more, she was deeply a part of us. We were not mad, we simply lacked the courage to speak about it as a film or about the directors. *Liz* was a spirit, the spirit of our lives. We had been too much a part of her life for too long. Liz had become us. There was nothing else that we were interested in.

That night and the next day we stayed with Liz by the small coffin. The scarecrow, having completely lost any sense of reason, whispered into my ear, 'We are here . . . We are here, and she is not on her own.'

When the child was buried, we stayed with Liz at the side of the freshly dug grave. I went to bed, while the scarecrow stayed. She refused to leave and kept crying.

Then, after some rest, I went back to replace her. And in such a way we kept up a rota, because Liz *shouldn't stay on her own.*

'See, she sits and doesn't move.' The scarecrow pointed her finger at Liz as I entered the auditorium. 'She's been sitting there for three hours. I worry that she won't survive this.'

'She . . .'

'No, never! Not this! No!'

And for the first time in our life together it was she who fell upon my chest, not I on hers. I held her, not knowing what to do.

And then I grew scared. I couldn't imagine life without Liz. It was the most horrible idea. *What then*? Everything would tumble down, our whole life, everything. We were nothing without Liz.

'I hope . . . I just hope she isn't going to . . .' The scarecrow was crying loudly. For the whole hour, Liz had been sitting all by herself in her flat gazing at the gas cooker.

As the scarecrow left, she whispered in my ear. 'Please watch her, I beg you, keep watching.' And I remained on my own. My heart beat like a mallet in the silence. An hour later Liz went to the bathroom and began to tie a washing line to a nail. I rushed around the auditorium. I didn't know what to do; there was a wall between us – that was the most horrific thing. I could see everything but could do *nothing*. And the scarecrow would not be back for five hours. I froze in horror. What would I tell her? She would come in nervously, ready in advance to disbelieve her eyes and ears. I could already hear my wooden voice, which would push me over into the abyss. 'Liz is no more. Liz is no more.'

I knew no words more horrible than those. The name 'Liz' only suited the word 'existence'. Only that. I rushed around, getting caught on the chairs. Liz was already knotting the washing line to the ceiling, above the cistern. Unable to hold myself back, I threw myself at the screen.

Liz, whose head reached the ceiling, put the washing line around her neck.

I began to scratch the screen, hitting it with my fists, aiming at her legs. Then, all my strength left me, and I slumped to my knees. I don't remember what happened; I was screaming like a madman.

'Liz, Liz! Don't do it! I beg you! Liz, please live! Don't do it! Please!'

I rushed around hysterically, but she had already climbed onto the toilet seat, and I curled into a ball, closing my ears and covering my eyes. I didn't want to know anything more, or to see anything more. I covered my face with my palms. This was the end. *The end.* The film that was supposed to never end, was ending.

When I came back to my senses and stood up, somebody was speaking in the auditorium. I turned around frantically. There was nobody there. I ran, then, along the rows of seats. I couldn't believe my ears, or my happiness. Liz was still *alive, still existed*, was standing in the doorway, and there, on the landing, stood a woman who was speaking (I couldn't hear what she was saying).

It wasn't important who the woman was, I was ready to kiss her feet. Just so long as she didn't leave.

It took a while for me to come back fully to my senses and sit down on the nearest seat. Finally, then, I could listen to the conversation.

'Why?'

'I don't want to.'

'Please, I'm pleading with you,' the woman said. 'Please, Liz.'

'Go away!' Liz screamed angrily.

'You're out of your mind. You are beside yourself.'

'Don't stick your nose into my life! Get lost!'

She slammed the door and, shaking all over, headed back to the bathroom. I jumped up immediately, feeling the sweat break out on my forehead. Why had she let her close the door? Why wasn't she knocking? Why wasn't she calling somebody? Did the woman not realise?

I wanted to run, to call people, I wanted to be there instead of that woman. But I . . . I wasn't able to do that. I . . . I realised that I was in an auditorium, an empty auditorium. But still . . . It felt as if somebody was tearing me to pieces. The tension was appalling. I felt I might faint at any moment. For the second time I had to watch as she climbed onto the toilet seat and reached for the washing line. I had to live through it again. No. I couldn't.

Suddenly the doorbell rang. I sensed the tension subside. Relief flooded me. Of course, the woman had come back. Look how *insistently* she was ringing the bell. Thank God. At that moment I would have given her everything, everything I had.

'What now?'

'I'm sorry, Liz, I can't leave.'

'What do you want?' Sweat was streaming down Liz's face, her body was shaking.

'I'm coming in,' the woman said.

'No!' She stood in her way.

'Why don't you want to let me in?'

'It's very late now!'

'Why are you shouting?'

'Leave me alone!'

Again, she attempted to slam the door, but this time the woman (well done!) pushed her foot into the doorway.

'I said let me in!' the woman said roughly, and unexpectedly Liz stepped back.

'Don't go in there!' Now she *pleaded* gently.

'Why?'

'Just please, don't.'

'What's in there?' the woman asked, in the hall now. 'Did you want to do something to yourself?'

'No, no.' She was nearly crying now.

'So what then? Why don't you want me to go in there?'

'I just don't!' she shouted, her voice tearful.

'Let me!'

And the woman headed for the kitchen, leaving Liz at the door. On the way she stopped suddenly by the bathroom door, rooted to the ground, and shuddered. Liz looked at her, frightened.

'What is this?' the woman said, suddenly, pointing at the washing line tied to the tank. 'What is this, I'm asking you?'

She ran up to Liz and began to slap her around the face with all her strength.

Liz's head swayed from side to side, as if dead. And then she broke into a terrible sob. At the same moment the woman, having stopped hitting Liz, began to sob too, falling down on her knees. She crouched there on all fours, like an animal, in a repulsive position, crying so hard that her tears fell like peas onto the floor.

'Oh, Liz, Liz,' she said, crying. And for some reason, she remained on all fours.

And Liz, kneeling down next to her, hugged the woman round her waist and they sobbed together, her head upon the woman's back.

My face was wet with tears too, and not having any strength left to watch any longer, I left the auditorium.

It was around three in the morning. The cool air caressed my chest and my face. The dark, gloomy street disappeared around a corner. I suddenly felt as if I had woken up. I looked around. Where was I? As if I didn't come here every day. Such a strange feeling came over me. What was I doing?

It was like those moments once a month at night when I was in the auditorium and I remembered *where I was from*. No, not that. It was not just that I remembered. There, in that lonely darkness, in a street lit by just one street light, I felt suddenly that I was trapped in some kind of nightmare. With Liz. With the scarecrow. What was this? I couldn't understand. My suffering, at that moment, felt so intense. Why? What was I living for?

I glanced at the patch of sky visible above the buildings where the stars glistened. It was a real nightmare. I needed to sleep. To go home. Where else could I go? Everything would fall into place. *I didn't understand what I was doing there.*

Out of nowhere, I experienced a long-forgotten feeling of freedom awaken within me. The scarecrow, my ordinary life, Liz – it all felt like an oppressive dream, a spell. I examined myself carefully again. The chains that had fastened me to that nightmare just five minutes before were gone. I felt so light. But I was exhausted, and my nerves were raw.

Laughing quietly, I walked on into the night mist. Of course I knew that the scarecrow would be home before long and that I would not be there. I knew that. But I doubted now that she was real, and that dampened the voice of my conscience. Obviously, I remembered how much I had suffered, the exhausting struggles I had lived through. But you can suffer in a dream too, can't you? Of course you can. Absolutely. You can suffer so much more in a dream than you do in real life.

Whistling quietly, I wandered through the deserted nocturnal city. No, it was impossible. Why would I, a husband, a father, a grandfather, wander around at night unsure where I was and why? What could they think about me? I realised I was the victim of hallucinations; I had read about it happening. Perhaps I was a lunatic? A film that never ends. What nonsense! A little cinema. Ridiculous! The scarecrow. Rubbish! It was all just nonsense!

I felt more joyful and lighter than I had for a long time. I could think *soberly*. Finally, I could think soberly like anybody else, and that awakened in me such a feeling of confidence and a thirst for life – for the kind of life that earlier had seemed so miserable and incomprehensible. To be *just* a man, *just* a husband, *just* a grandfather. What else could I need? At that moment I really did not want to experience any earth-shattering feelings; why would I? I was too tired. I wanted to be like everybody else, sober and free of nightmares. God, why did I need secrets? I was tired of them. I was tired of suffering. I wanted to believe in reality, with no secrets; the reality of everybody else's lives. How simple people's lives were; they worried about money and their careers. They earned their money and sat around the table together, happy and joking. And what did those other feelings mean to them? What did they mean at all? God, how jealous I was of their lightness, their simplicity.

I was right by my home when suddenly, exhausted by my thoughts, I felt strangely nervous and stopped. The scarecrow, having gone to the cinema and finding that I was not there, would be rushing around like mad, crawling on all fours, sobbing, looking for me beneath the seats, running up and down the street, calling for me tearfully. I had to hurry back to her – to save her.

It took all my will-power to stop myself. What was the matter with me? How could I believe that? I was grey-haired. The sobriety that had filled me with joy an hour before (I so missed it), told me that there *could be no such thing* as the small cinema, or the scarecrow. No man in his right mind would ever believe there was. I was sick if I believed it. I was just ill. I would go to the doctor the next day and tell him everything; he would prescribe some pills, and everything would pass.

I smiled and took out the key. When I got to the third floor I wasn't even surprised when, turning it in the lock, it clicked open. The flat was dark, and not wanting to wake the others, I lay down on the sofa in the living room. And soon after, I nodded off.

How long it had been since I had felt such bliss! I was at home, with my family. My beloved ones slept on the other side of the wall. Those people who were closest to me. I had never left; it was just an enchantment, a heavy dream that had lasted a couple of hours, though it felt like many years.

I would tell them everything and we would all laugh. They would help me heal. I would love my wife and my daughter and my granddaughter. I would live with them. I would lose myself in them and would find myself in them. Finally.

It was morning when I was woken by a terrible scream.

'Mum! Mum! He came back!'

When I opened my eyes, I was confused. My daughter was standing in the doorway, in her nightie, her eyes full of horror. I smiled at her and attempted to sit up. By the time I was sitting, my wife was stood in the doorway too, also in her nightie, along with the lanky guy with a plait (I had forgotten about him) who was in his pyjamas. And then there was another middle-aged man I didn't know, with a big hairy belly, wearing only his underpants. I had no idea how they could all fit in the same doorway. I attempted a smile as I looked at them. They didn't move an inch.

'What are you doing here?' My wife stepped forward, suddenly, her voice raised. 'What have you come for, you old lecher? Nobody wants you here.'

Still smiling, I stood up.

'You must understand,' I explained to my wife, growing numb with fear. 'It all was just a dream. I'm ill, Raja. Probably very ill.'

'And back then? You weren't ill then?'

'When?'

'Then, you old womaniser, when you left Nurochka and me with the baby! When we so desperately needed your support!'

'I . . . You don't understand,' I whispered. 'It was painful for me. I'm not a lecher. I didn't want to.'

'Aha! He didn't want to.' My wife dug her fists into her sides. 'Just look at him! Now that he's had enough of sleeping around with teenagers he's crawled back. You degenerate! What's the matter, has your willy withered? What are you staring at?' She addressed the man. 'What are you looking at, Zenia? You haven't seen him before, have you? Well, just admire him!'

'He's drunk,' my daughter said. 'He's just drunk. Look how he's smiling and swaying. Like a drunk.'

'I just told you that. I know that!' My wife shouted again. 'I knew God would punish him. For everything. For the shame he brought on us. For his filth. I knew it!'

'Well, Mister, it's time for you to be on your way.'

The unknown man with a big hairy belly, who had so far stood quietly behind their backs, pushed apart those in the doorway and came over to me.

'Well.'

'I won't go anywhere,' I said, closing my eyes. 'This is my home, my family.'

'He's gone mad!' I heard another male voice and immediately felt somebody grip my elbow firmly.

'Well!'

'I'm not going! I have nowhere to go!' I pressed my feet to the floor with all my strength.

'For goodness sake, what are you waiting for?' I heard my wife's irritated voice. 'Can't you just throw the old drunkard out?'

They began to drag me out into the corridor.

Suddenly I heard a child's voice.

'Granddad! Granddad! Don't! I'm afraid!'

A child's cry followed, turning everything inside me upside down. Struggling with all my might, I freed myself from their hands and rushed to my granddaughter. The only one for whom I existed.

'My baby!'

'Granddad!' She let out a frenzied scream seeing me running towards her.

There was something in her voice that made me stop. The next moment the girl leapt towards the man with the big belly, grabbing hold of his fat hairy legs.

'Granddad, granddad, I'm afraid of him!' she muttered through her tears, pointing towards me. 'He's scary!'

'Just get lost!' The lanky guy with the plait pushed me in the back. 'Just get out of our home!'

Having grabbed me by the scruff of my neck, like a dog, he pushed me out onto the landing.

'Swine!'

He slammed the door.

For a moment I stood, stunned. And then something in me churned up a memory of Nura as a little girl hugging me at the seaside. 'Dad, Daddy! Can you hear me? The waves are louder than me. I love you!' The waves are louder than me. The three of us: me, my wife and Nura, there, by the sea, on the beach.

I sat in the corner and sobbed quietly, unable to bear the cracks in time.

I stood up, then, not feeling myself, and then suddenly I smiled. Yes, I smiled like I had the time before when I had left the flat. Of course, I had got lost, that would explain it. This was *not my* daughter, *not my* wife and *not my* granddaughter. That was the answer. And that easily the suffering of my soul was eased. I had lost my way. They mistook me for somebody else, which explained why they were so insulting. It had nothing to do with me.

Still smiling, I descended the stairs. My wife and my daughter loved me. Those, the distant ones. I had a daughter, a real daughter who *loved* me. She was waiting for me, the poor thing, in the cinema.

It was a dream. I walked through the city, which was already waking. It was, of course, a dream; what had happened in the flat was nothing more than a horrible oppressive dream.

I was too weak to tell the difference between dream and reality.

She was waiting for me in her place, at the back by the wall. The scarecrow. She rushed towards me (old and stumbling) the moment she saw me in the doorway. By what miracle did she sense what had happened to me?

'You poor thing, my poor thing!' she called as she hurried towards me. 'They insulted you again!'

'How did you know?'

'I can feel it. It's in your face.'

She squeezed me in her slim arms and held me. She cried quietly, compassionately. And once more she soothed my pain with her mad pity.

'You know . . .' I whispered. 'They . . . I got lost. It wasn't my daughter.'

'I'm your daughter,' the scarecrow whispered.

'You're my daughter, I know,' I replied.

'Don't go there. Ever. There is no place for us there.'

'Yes.'

'You can carry on working on your cabinet. Let's go home.'

'Oh, the cabinet.'

I smiled and sighed. She stroked me everywhere, wherever she could, soothing my pain.

'Look.'

I lifted up my head and looked at the screen. Liz. How could I forget her? *Our Liz.*

She was sleeping, in her bed, twitching nervously in her dream. Beside her, fully naked, slept the woman.

'Wait,' I said, pushing away from the scarecrow. 'You don't know what happened.'

'They . . .' the scarecrow whispered. 'You know?'

'Do you know what happened?'

'I know. When I came, Liz was lying almost unconscious, with that woman kissing her and stroking her. They looked like they were crazy.'

'Why?'

'The tears had made them weak. They *didn't care*, you know?'

'They . . .'

'Yes, they saved themselves.'

'But *Liz* . . .'

'You know, she had suffered so much. She just felt how she was being kissed. And then she nodded off. She didn't even realize that she had nodded off. She didn't really understand anything that happened.'

'Why are there wine glasses?'

'Which? They drank vodka.'

'From wine glasses?'

'They're both *drunk*,' the scarecrow whispered. 'It's easier that way.'

She dragged me home.

I don't know how many years passed. Life carried on for me and the scarecrow. During that time, I constructed eight out of the ten drawers and soon, very soon, the cabinet for the bathroom, my *master work*, would be finished.

I felt light again. Rarely did I think about where I had come from. And so it was as if my pain had never existed. Only occasionally would I bump into *not-my*-wife in town, with *not-my*-daughter. Then a pale smile would illuminate my face.

To be honest, the reason I bumped into them was because I would wait for them near their house. I don't know why I so needed that; to observe them from a distance. They were always rushing somewhere. And then I would smile to myself and walk away unnoticed.

As I recall, I spoke to my daughter only *once*. She happened to walk close by me *on her own*, totally *alone* one early autumnal morning. I couldn't hold myself back. I stepped out from behind the tree.

'Oh!' She cried and stopped, pressing her handbag to her chest. 'You're stalking us.'

'No,' I answered quietly, embarrassed. 'Nura, I wanted . . .'

'Let me go!'

'Go, I'm not stopping you. I just wanted . . .'

I thought she would walk away. She was always so rude to me. But now . . . Yes, now she was on her own, without the family, without her husband, or her mother, or her daughter, in that alleyway. For some reason she did not walk away, though I did nothing to stop her.

'Nura,' I said quietly, not looking at her. 'I'm your father. I loved you, you know. Do you remember, by the seaside? Do you remember?'

'Dad, don't!' she said angrily.

And then I began to weep.

'We don't need all this!' she said, angry again, opening and closing her bag nervously. 'Why are you crying? I thought you never cried. I didn't know you knew how to cry.'

I couldn't bear the way she said, 'Dad'. It was true, *never, not a single time* had they seen me cry, no matter how difficult life had been. I don't know why.

'Dad, please, don't,' my daughter said, a twitch in her voice.

'But you do remember, don't you, Nura?' I asked. 'Do you remember when the three of us . . .'

'Dad, you are tearing apart my heart. You've changed. You're different. You can't bring back the past. You . . .'

'No, Nura, no,' I said. 'I'm the same. It was all a terrible mistake. I can't stand it.'

'What mistake? You dumped us.'

'I didn't dump you . . . No, I . . . It was so difficult for me. I felt so lonely.'

'Why?'

'I don't know. You all . . . I felt so redundant.'

'When?'

'Then. You didn't notice anything. I wanted to be with you, I did. I . . .'

'I find it difficult to understand you,' my daughter said. 'I'm in a hurry, I've got lots of things to do.'

She was about to walk away.

'But you remember? Tell me. You loved me, didn't you, there, by the sea?'

'Yes, Dad. Yes!' she said angrily. 'And so what?'

'I'm the same!' I shouted as she walked away. 'Remember, I'm the same! Please understand me!'

She walked away, annoyed, and, it seemed to me, a little confused. From that day, I never again thought of the scarecrow as my daughter.

In the meantime, *Liz*, our *Liz*, got married. For the second time. The woman who had saved her was the witness. The scarecrow and I also prepared for the celebration. It was a modest but proper wedding. We didn't envy Liz's middle-aged man with a tie, sitting to her left.

'I'm so happy, so happy,' the scarecrow whispered, pouring some champagne for herself and me. 'She deserved it, she deserved happiness. Thank God.'

'She doesn't love him,' I said looking at Liz's eyes, which were not full of joy. 'She could only love that one, remember? Serioza.'

'She loved him, but she suffered with him,' whispered the scarecrow. 'She has been alone for so long. Now she will have some support in her life. That's the most important thing.'

'He's an accountant.'

'She doesn't need a star plucked from heaven, you know. She's tired.'

'How will they live?' I asked.

'She will have a child again, you'll see.'

We toasted Liz. When they all shouted, 'Kiss the bride!' we too shouted quietly.

The wedding night that Saturday coincided with our planned monthly nocturnal visit to see Liz, but the scarecrow protested.

'Let's postpone it. It's their wedding night. I couldn't.'

'But it isn't their first night,' I said.

'Still.'

I didn't insist. We visited her again at night two weeks later. The first thing we saw was her new husband kissing her face, while Liz lay there looking as if she was made of stone.

Then everything repeated itself, like in a dream. She gave birth to a boy, and again it was Serioza's child. Yes, Liz shocked us and brought us joy. Sometimes she could be incredibly practical. During those two weeks we stayed with her not for the two hours we normally did, but for five. They were fatal weeks for her. She had arranged a business trip to the town of S, where Serioza lived. And there, flirtatious, employing all her charms, she conquered his pain and his anger and seduced him. For the second time. And that evening, he let down his defences again. In the morning, having got what she wanted, she disappeared.

For a long time, I couldn't understand why she needed it to be that way. Why did she not want to have a child with her husband? But then, I thought, perhaps I did understand.

She wanted to hold on to the *blood-ties* from her past, and, more importantly, to *repeat* her life, and with that repetition *to drown* her former pain. It was that simple. Because, otherwise, why was she so happy to know she was going to have a son again? And why, immediately, without giving it a second thought, did she give him *the same* name? Her visits to the grave grew less frequent then, and she began to catch busses that didn't go past the cemetery. The baby looked just like the first one, the dead one. Which was not surprising really; they were both the child of the same mother and father. And then, when he *reached the age the first one had been*, she stopped visiting the grave altogether. And why, at that moment, did she *stop communicating* with the woman who had saved her life? For no reason at all.

Liz – the scarecrow and I continued to live with her. As always, I carried on making dinner for the scarecrow; I washed her while she splashed around like a cat. I combed her hair as she purred. I grew used to her long nose. She was like a big animal in my house, nothing more. In my lonely life. She was not a woman at all. A large animal, which at times, when my heart felt like it was breaking from the pain, would hug the already ancient me with her arms and legs and cry with me, *pitying* me.

What happened then was unexpected, like everything that had happened in my life. I struggled out of bed, coughing. I was wrinkled and very advanced in years. Liz was old, too, her face visibly creased. That day I was due to go to see Liz on my own. The scarecrow had to go to the doctor; she had a pain in her side. The scarecrow was still full of vitality. The night before I had had a strange dream. My old family, who I had almost forgotten, came to me and asked for my forgiveness. Especially my daughter, who had long been divorced from her husband. Having experienced bitterness herself, she kept begging me, 'Come back to us, Dad. Come.' And my old wife smiled, leniently, alone in the corner.

I got up and went to see Liz, leaning on my stick. The cinema was the same. How many years had passed? And the people who came and went as quietly as shadows, they were the same too. If visibly older. The boy in the sweater was grey. Did he also live Liz's life? I didn't know. Liz belonged to us, the scarecrow and me, nobody else. I tried not to think about those other people.

But that day there was not a soul around. When I entered the auditorium, having slotted a coin into the machine, I knew right away that something was wrong. I felt sick and my legs were weak. I hoped I wasn't about to die. It wasn't that I cared particularly; the only thing that still breathed some life into me were my old memories of the seaside. That and the knowledge that the scarecrow worried about me.

I sat in my seat and, for a long time, watched a funeral, not really comprehending much of what I saw. The funeral was for some old woman. Behind the hearse walked a woman, holding a bent man by his elbow. And, beside them, another old woman.

Then I heard the voices of the mourners, but I was not interested in listening to what they were talking about. Somebody had died suddenly. Somebody. I didn't care who it was.

I went out into the street. It was a bright summer's day. From far away I saw a woman walking towards me. Leaning on my stick, I watched as she drew closer.

'Is that you?' I asked, recognizing Liz. It was Liz. She was old, nearly as old as the woman in the hearse, among the wreaths.

'It's me,' she smiled. 'Let's go.'

'Let's go.'

I didn't ask her where. I didn't care.

The actress playing Liz had stepped out of the screen, the moment she died. How? It was her, of course. She walked in front of me, turning occasionally and stopping to wait for me.

There was a car around the corner, with a man I didn't know behind the wheel.

'Get in.'

I sat in the back, with Liz next to me. The car moved forward.

I couldn't believe my eyes; she was next to me. She was *real.* It was her. Liz. The woman I had shared my life with. Not able to hold myself back, I took hold of her hand. She smiled at me knowingly. Clutching onto her wrist, I felt her pulse.

There was a crowd of people waiting when we arrived at a patch of waste ground. Somebody was being buried. I recognised the people, it was the same procession. Up above somebody moved on a crane, filming the scene.

No longer surprised by anything, I wriggled out of the car. Liz, standing on the other side, smiled and shouted unexpectedly.

'Hey! Hey! He's here! He's here already!'

The whole procession turned towards me. They encircled me in a tight circle. They spoke, laughed, smiled in a friendly way, touching me with their hands.

I took Liz's hand.

'Liz,' I whispered. 'Who is there, in the hearse?'

'A mannequin,' Liz said.

'I have lived for you. From the time you were . . .'

'I know.'

'Liz.' I was afraid she might not hear me. 'The film that never ends . . .'

'It has ended. For you it has ended.'

She smiled and took off a grey wig. A waterfall of black hair fell down upon her shoulders. And then, putting her fingers into her mouth, she pulled out the rotten teeth, together with an artificial jaw and I saw a girl's teeth, as white as snow. From inside her dress she took out two small pillows; the large breasts of the old woman grew attractively small. Finally, somebody passed her a carafe of water and there, in front of me, she washed away her wrinkles and the paleness from her skin.

I recognised Liz, the one I had met many years before, the one who had quarrelled with her mother about a trip to Spain. Young, passionate, pink-cheeked.

'Liz,' I said. 'Did you go actually go to Spain that time?'

The girl just laughed merrily and hugged me.

'Liz . . .' I said. 'I . . .'

I didn't have time to say anything more. I was hoisted up into their arms and they began to carry me above their heads, laughing, joyful, spinning around like madmen. From the height I was, it was probably only I who saw the hearse with the mannequin, forgotten by everybody else.

Liz, Liz, wash the wrinkles from my face too. Take off my balding wig. Liz, you have been everything to me. I want to live a different life, Liz. I . . . Liz, you didn't get old. You didn't die, no, it's a mannequin that lies there. No, I didn't die. It's only a film.

The scarecrow sat in the cinema by herself. Seeing how they carried me on their shoulders, dancing, shouting, their voices merry, she suppressed a quiet sob.

'Poor you, my poor little thing. How wonderful for you,' she whispered.

If you enjoyed this,
why not try some more Lithuanian novels?

Breathing into Marble

By Laura Sintija Cerniauskaite

Winner of the European Prize for Literature

When Isabel decides to adopt the troubled young orphan, Ilya, she has no idea of the trauma that is about to be unleashed upon her family. Taking him back home to their cottage in the country, his dark presence unsettles the family and resurrects the ghosts of Isabel's past.

Breathing into Marble is a dark and poetic story of love, family, deception and death.

'Černiauskaitė could be a major talent of this generation; her prose puts some of our intellectual writers to shame.' *World Literature Today*

The Easiest

By Rasa Askinyte

Blanca works at Café France. If she actually exists. There she meets the characters of the novel, Alex and Not-Alex, Greek, the owner of the café and Anastasia her best friend. It is a story of love, of not loving and of an apartment reached only by a ladder and birds that come crashing down onto table tops.

Askinyte's novel is lightly and lyrically told, but beneath the surface bubbles a dark and disturbing world.

Shtetl Love Song

By Grigory Kanovich

'I had intended for quite a long time to write about my mother with that joyous enthusiasm and abundant detail with which it is fitting to recall one's parents, the people closest and dearest to you.'

In *Shtetl Love Song* Grigory Kanovich writes about his mother, and in so doing peels back the surface of the rich Yiddish community that lived in pre-war Lithuania.

It is a requiem for the pre-war Jewish shtetl, for a people and a way of life that was destroyed in the maelstrom of war.

Compan

Revised Comn

2. All Age Worship Year A

Already published

Companion to the Revised Common Lectionary
1: Intercessions

Julie M. Hulme

Companion to the Revised Common Lectionary

2. All Age Worship Year A

EPWORTH PRESS

0 7162 0522 X

First Published 1998
by Epworth Press
20 Ivatt Way
Peterborough, PE3 7PG

Typeset by Regent Typesetting, London
Printed and bound in Great Britain by
Biddles Ltd, Guildford and King's Lynn

Contents

This book is dedicated to the memory
of the
Revd D. Mary Holliday
(1923–1997)

Introduction

God is love.
God loves you – me – us.
Prayer is that openness of heart and mind which allows us to accept God's love for us and offer ourselves to it.
God is always present and always ready to meet with us.
We surrender to the glory of God as God yearns to be revealed through us and in all things.
In our surrender, we learn how to live within the love of God and be transformed by it.
And God-in-us meets and transforms the world.

Prayer then is essentially very simple. And yet, because we are complex, multi-layered personalities, it is often very difficult to pray. Our bodies are tense, our emotions are unstable, our minds wander or are daunted by the scale of the world's pain – and in the depths of our souls we battle with a deep reluctance born of guilt and shame, anger and fear. In our fragmented state we are not conscious of any peace for ourselves, or any blessing for others. At such times, it is only by faith that we can continue in prayer at all.

All prayer is a receiving or an offering – or both. It is like answering the door. Getting to the door can be hard work in itself, but what follows is utterly beyond our control. For the knock at the door is the wild wind of the Spirit, the Lover and Stranger who desires not only communion with us, but our companionship on an unpredictable journey. And so we struggle with prayer not least because we are awed at what is asked of us.

This being so – how do we go about leading prayer in corporate worship? How dare we attempt it? We do so by remembering not our frailty but the One who is present to us in our praying. It is God's love and grace which make prayer possible: God's desire to meet us for communion, healing and joy; and our faith in that even when all else fails us.

God is the source and spring of our praying together. Any moment when we meet to pray is a space marked out for God's purposes. The beginning of an act of worship takes us over a threshold into the place of encounter. What follows happens at God's initiative. The 'life-giving' quality of worship does not lie in its content as such but in the extent to which those taking part yield the time and the content to God. Liturgy or free praise? Hymns or choruses? Written or extempore prayer? All these distinctions are, in the end, irrelevant. What matters is that whatever is offered is *offered*, that is, in the hearts of the worshippers surrendered to God.

For the preacher or leader of worship, there is a very strong temptation to keep hold, to retain control, to resist surrendering the offering because we are afraid of what will happen if we let it go. But the renewal of the Body of Christ begins with the humility with which we prepare worshippers for such a direct and transforming encounter, help them interpret what is going on, provide signposts guiding them through, and enable them later to step back into the narrative of their daily lives. The imagery, structure and rhythm of our verbal praying supplies this framework, assisted by the readings, hymns and other elements of the service. Yet the real prayer is what the congregation offers *within* this framework.

So the structure must be sufficient, without becoming an obstacle. Leading public prayer is a task to be undertaken with gentleness, as the outbreathing of a love so tender that it does not break a bruised reed or quench a flickering flame. As far as possible, we must not place ourselves between the people and their Lord. The words exist to stimulate a response, not to us, but *to God*, so imagination, creativity and risk must be submitted to our loving knowledge of the congregation with whom we pray.

On the other hand, we must avoid clichés, and that excessive caution which stifles the Spirit by defining too closely what an image should mean. Our knowledge of Christian theology is the foundation of our praying, not its *life*. Prayer is always pushing at the limits of words because God is not only in our words but beyond them, and we are bringing each other to the point of surrender into that unknown.

Our corporate praying has to be built around what at first seems to be an empty space. We do not *fill* this silence with words: rather, we *create* it with word-structures, word-pictures, spoken, sung or chanted rhythms, and with story. This space is larger than the words themselves and reaches into an infinity which is within, between and yet beyond us.

All our verbal or written prayers are working towards that moment when together we step off the edge into the abyss which is the wordless, soundless, endless love of God in Christ. Once we have made that step, we are no longer in control. But we are surrendered to the love which holds us, feeds us, heals us, renews us; and sends us out as seeds of fire to light the world.

Julie M. Hulme
February 1998

Using this book

The readings on which this book is based are from the Revised Common Lectionary Year A, as adapted for use by preachers in the Methodist Church, but as great care has been taken to draw out major images and themes in the material, I hope that it will be useful to those who are following other lectionaries, as well as those who order their worship in other ways.

An authorized lectionary is, in one sense, an embodiment of the church's response to the Word of God. It is one way in which the ancient and universal church speaks to the local congregation, passing on what it has 'received from the Lord'. The Revised Common Lectionary contains a vast amount of material, including numerous 'optional' readings. While remaining faithful to the seasons of the Christian year, the Lectionary also provides great scope for those preachers and congregations who wish to read scripture in sequence. In editing and writing this book, I have tried to provide preachers with a flexible and practical tool which will give them a door into this embarrassment of riches and which will go some way towards reconciling the needs of those who prefer sequential readings, and those who prefer a 'thematic' approach.

In doing so, I have had to simplify the material in a number of ways. For example, the Lectionary contains readings for both morning and evening: the readings quoted in this book are drawn from the morning only. Over Christmas, and in Holy Week, the full lectionary includes a much wider range of readings than those listed here. Selecting is subjective and restrictive, but I have tried to offset this with an extensive thematic index and suggestions for prayers which might be used on festivals which are not covered in detail (see Appendix 3).

There is a section for each Sunday of the year, plus the major Christian festivals which fall mid-week, reflecting the growing importance of mid-week worship. The titles and themes are suggestions for those preachers who need an 'entry point' into the material, but the prayers relate to the readings themselves, not just to the theme. The suggestions for illustrating the theme are not fully worked through in terms of presentation and often consist of a series of questions. They are intended to give an idea of how the diverse nuances of the readings might be brought together into a coherent whole, and what issues arising from the text might need to be addressed. An attempt has been made to provide a strong visual theme for each week.

These prayers have been written for use with people of all ages, which means that, generally speaking, the construction, language and thought-forms have been kept fairly simple without avoiding 'long words' altogether. There is a strong emphasis on symbols and imagery, on congregational responses and on the use of rhythm and repetition. Although, following the practice of Jesus, God is still addressed as 'Father', other forms of address are explored, including some which respect the feminine in the divine. The imagery of light has been retained, but the 'light = good, dark = evil' dichotomy has been avoided wherever possible.

For any given Sunday, the book probably contains more material than can be used in a particular service: the aim has been to pay attention to the different elements of prayer and give the preacher maximum choice in how they should be put together. In combining elements, such as Adoration-Confession-Thanksgiving it is worth reflecting on how the space between the prayers might be used – the insertion of silence or music at these points can enhance the whole. Although each prayer stands alone, most of them have been written so that they can be used together in this way – and not just those where this is indicated in the text. It is for this reason that concluding phrases such as 'through Jesus Christ our Lord' have been omitted.

Suggestions are given in each section for a Call to Worship, but to be fair, they do not all contain the element of 'call', some being rather a thematic introduction or heading. Prayers of Adoration, Confession and Thanksgiving follow. Sometimes the element of penitence is served by a Prayer of Acknowledgment which is less to do with individual confession and more concerned with our general awareness of the pain and evil present in our community and the world. Declarations of Forgiveness are implicit in some prayers, and some of the Prayers of Thanksgiving can be used in this way, but where a more specific declaration is needed, suggestions can be found in Appendix 1.

Similarly, prayers relating the seasonal readings to Communion have been included in Appendix 2, in order to reflect not just the growing importance of the Eucharist in Sunday and midweek worship, but also the trend towards including children in the celebration.

Prayers of Intercession are not included, as these are the subject of the first book in this series, but many of the Prayers of Petition could be used as part of intercessory prayers if required.

The Prayers of Dedication have been written to fulfil a variety of needs: they can be used after Confession, or as a response to the Word, or to conclude prayers of intercession, or at the dedication of the offering. The Prayers of Dismissal serve not only to bless the departing congregation but also commission it for service in the world. There are a number of Meditations scattered throughout the book, some of which are more complex in form, and repay careful reading.

Contributors

I am grateful to a number of contributors who have collaborated with me in writing prayers or in supplying ideas which I developed. The numbers indicate the prayers for which they should receive credit:

DAVID BAGWELL is a Methodist minister whose responsibilities include a 'church plant' – joint Anglican–Methodist LEP involving regular all-age worship with 'unchurched' families. 241, 243, 245, 250, 251, 252, 255, 256, 257,258, 263, 264, 265, 268, 269, 270, 431, 432, 438.

PATRICIA BATSTONE was accredited as a Methodist local preacher in 1964. She is a freelance writer, poet and editor with experience in teaching and bookselling. 113, 117, 120, 121, 123, 124, 125, 126, 127, 129, 130, 131, 133, 135, 136, 137, 138, 140, 141, 143, 144.

STEVEN BROWNING is a Methodist minister and university chaplain. He has experience of an Anglican–Methodist 'church plant' and a keen interest in the development of community liturgy. 332, 334, 338, 339, 344, 349, 355, 441, 442.

TIM CROME is a Methodist minister with extensive experience of work on housing estates with 'inner city' problems. His current responsibilities include an Anglican-Methodist congregation which meets in a community centre. He has served as chaplain to The Queen's College, Birmingham. 304, 305,307, 309, 311, 312, 315, 316, 317, 318, 319, 321, 322, 323,324, 327, 328, 329, 434, 436.

ALBERT GAYLE is a Methodist minister with experience of prison chaplaincy and work in schools. He is a member of the Ordinands' Retreat Leadership team. 273, 274, 275, 276, 277, 278, 279, 283, 284, 285, 291, 292, 294, 295, 297, 298, 300, 301, 424.

PAULINE GREASLEY is a primary school teacher and a Methodist local preacher, with interests in meditative prayer and creative worship for all ages. 1, 2, 4, 9, 11, 14, 16, 19, 21, 22, 24, 32, 34, 35, 38, 421, 422.

JANE LEACH is a Methodist minister with experience in midweek clubs for 'unchurched' children and work within schools. She enjoys working with families to develop accessible liturgies for baptisms,weddings and funerals. 185, 187,1]89, 191, 193, 194, 196, 198, 199, 200, 202, 204, 206, 209, 210, 212.

ALISON PEPPER currently works as a secretary and is the organist at her local Methodist church. With a background in theology, she has a growing interest in writing prayers and meditations which link personal experience with the worship of the local community. 49, 50, 52, 64, 72, 429.

FIRST SUNDAY OF ADVENT

Isaiah 2.1–5; Psalm 122; Romans 13.11–14; Matthew 24.36–44

AWAKENING TO LIGHT

Presentation

Illustration: an alarm clock. Do we find it easy to wake up in the morning? Or to stay awake when we need to be bright and alert? What do we use to help us? What do we miss – in creation, and in other people – if we are too dull or self-centred to look around us? Are we in danger of missing the new thing God is doing in the world?

(I) Call to Worship

Isaiah 2.2–3a, Psalm 122.1; *or the following:*
Read Romans 13. 11–12

Wake up! Wake up! **The light of a new dawn breaks.**
Get up! Get up! **Meet the light of the morning.**
Come, come now! **To meet the Lord of light on his earthward way.**

(2) Meditation

It has been night: now the sun rises,
bringing warmth and colour to the earth.
You are God: Creator and Lord of light,
bringing warmth and colour to our lives.
To all the world you give the promise of returning day:
to all the world you give the rainbow hope:
joy in orange, hope in green, peace in blue and love in red.
From the new brightness of Spring to the yellow ripening of Summer;
from the brown decay of Autumn, to the white sleep of Winter,
you are the beginning and the end, the everlasting God of hope,
life to all creation. May your name be praised in light!

This meditation could also be used as an act of thanksgiving, following prayers of confession.

(3) Prayer of Adoration

Lord, we enter your house of beauty,
to discover life and joy in your presence:
for the night is drawing to its close:
And the day is almost here.

Lord, we enter your house of peace,
to deepen our communion with each other:
for the night is drawing to its close:
And the day is almost here.

Lord, we enter your house of justice,
where all that is wrong will be found out:
for the night is drawing to its close:
And the day is almost here.

Lord, we enter your house of learning,
where the Spirit will lead us into all truth:
for the night is drawing to its close:
And the day is almost here.

Lord, we enter your house of love,
where with people from all lands, nations, cultures and tongues,
we can join with the saints who have gone before us
as one great congregation, gathered in praise:
for the night is drawing to its close:
And the day is almost here.

(4) Prayer of Confession

Living, loving, forgiving God, we are sorry for sleeping so long:
for our morning stupor that leaves us neither awake nor aware.
Lord, forgive our sleepiness, our sluggishness of mind.
Silence.

We are sorry for not being ready: that we were not prepared for you,
not expecting to meet you, here, or in other people's needs.
Lord, forgive our lateness and our lack of preparation.
Silence.

We are sorry for not being there when you called us to work for you:
to help, to listen, to love and to pray.
Lord, forgive our absence and our failure to respond.
Silence.

We are sorry we have not paid attention: we have been too easily distracted, too busy with our own affairs.
Lord, forgive our selfishness and our lack of care.
Silence.

We come in all humility to ask for your forgiveness:
Help us now to wake up, keep watch, and prepare your way.

(5) Prayer of Dedication

We praise you, God of unity,
for through the breadth and depth of your forgiveness,
we are reconciled to each other and to you.
Let us praise the God of love:
Come, let us walk in the light of the Lord.

We praise you, God of truth,
for you help us to see what is wrong, and put it right,
and you are at our side as we establish justice between individuals, peoples and nations.
Let us praise the God of love:
Come, let us walk in the light of the Lord.

We praise you, God of peace,
for you strengthen all those who live compassionately
in the midst of hatred, and who teach others to make peace.
Let us praise the God of love:
Come, let us walk in the light of the Lord.

(6) Prayer of Dismissal

Go out in faith, bearing the armour of light
for the cause of God's peace,
as people of love and truth and praise.

SECOND SUNDAY OF ADVENT

Isaiah 11.1–10; Psalm 72.1–7. 18–19; Romans 15.4–13; Matthew 3.1–12

PRUNED BY LOVE

Presentation
Illustration: pruning shears/drawing of a shaggy 'bush' with a main stem and many unnecessary branches, deadheads and leaves. Discuss: why do we prune roses, and fruiting plants and trees? To produce more and better fruit. List together: what faults and wrongs did the prophets wish to see 'pruned' out of the people? What needs to be pruned from our own lives? Consider how this is done by repentance, and obedience to the word of God. What fruit might we then expect to see?

(7) Call to Worship

Isaiah 11.1–3 *or* Psalm 72.18–19.

(8) Prayer of Adoration

O God of all life, you call us to a life of praise,
so that we may share your word of joy:
O God of life, we praise your holy name.

O God of all truth, you call us to a life of purity,
so that in our homes, our work, and our communities,
your word of holiness can bear fruit in justice:
O God of truth, we praise your holy name.

O God of love, you call us to a life of dedication,
so that at all times, and in all places,
your word of hope may be recognized and your glory praised:
O God of love, we praise your holy name.

(9) Prayer of Confession

Father, Gardener of all creation, we are your fruit trees.
Our yield is poor, so you come to prune away our dead wood.
And we are afraid
  of the pain; of open wounds; of infection;
  of new growth which will change our shape, stimulate new shoots, and make us bend with the weight of fruit.
We are afraid that your pruning will make us different.
We have been dormant too long
  satisfied with ourselves, maintaining the cycle of life, but not being productive.
Forgive us, Lord, and prune away our complacency.
Prune away our pride. Prune away . . . (*other faults can be added from your list*)
Silence.

Now you are making us into new trees; trees that will feel the light on their leaves, draw the rain through their roots, and be nourished by the Gardener's care. May we blossom and bear fruit for you.

(10) Prayer of Thanksgiving

Loving Jesus, Word of God, we thank you

- for becoming a child, so that we would see how vulnerable God could be;
- for teaching of love, so that we could learn of God's promise to us;
- for acting in mercy, so that we could be healed through faith and prayer;
- for being obedient even to death, so that we could be saved to the uttermost.

Loving Jesus, Word of God, we thank you for your life of humble love in our midst, and for the example of those who have followed you in every age. Encourage us in their hope. Unite us with them in your praise.

(11) Prayer of Petition

Judge eternal, Lord of mercy, Father of us all:
your children are crying in pain and despair.
Because of our greed, they cry out for food:
Let your children be fed.
Because of our hatreds, they cry out for peace:
Let your children have life.
Because of our oppression, they cry out for justice:
Let your children be free.
Because of our apathy, they cry out for tenderness:
Let your children sing for joy.
Judge eternal, look upon us with compassion.
Lord of mercy, heal the wounds of the world.
Father of us all, reach out to the cold, the hungry and the lost:
Your kingdom come.

Silence, then read Isaiah 11.1–10.
This is the word of the Lord: **Thanks be to God.**

(12) Prayer of Dedication

O God of love, in obedience to your Word,
may we welcome one another as Christ has welcomed us:
That your mercy may be praised throughout the earth.
May we serve one another as Christ has served us:
That your mercy may be praised throughout the earth.
May we reveal your truth and confirm the promises you have made:
That your mercy may be praised throughout the earth.
May we learn more of your steadfast compassion for all people:
That your mercy may be praised throughout the earth.
May we encourage each other, so that we are all built up in hope:
That your mercy may be praised throughout the earth.
May we live together in harmony, and give glory to you:
That your mercy may be praised throughout the earth.

(13) Prayer of Dismissal

Read Romans 15.5–6. Glory to God! **Glory to God!**
Read Romans 15.13. Glory to God! **Glory to God!**

THIRD SUNDAY OF ADVENT

Isaiah 35.1–10; Psalm 146.5–10; James 5.7–10; Matthew 11.2–11

PREPARING THE WAY

Presentation

Illustration: 'Roadworks' signs, spades, wheelbarrow, bucket, models of bulldozers etc. Why do we need people to repair the road – even if we don't use cars? What are the difficulties and hazards of a bad road? And the advantages of a good one? If well-built and well-repaired roads are necessary for safe travel and good communications, what does it mean for us to 'prepare the highway' for God?

(14) Call to Worship

Isaiah 35.3–4 *or* Psalm146.1–2, 10; *or the following:*

Prepare the way for the Lord!
Make straight paths for him!
Every valley shall be raised up;
Every mountain and hill made low;
the rough ground shall become level,
And the rugged places a plain.
The glory of the Lord will be revealed.
Prepare the way!

(15) Prayer of Adoration

O God of deliverance, we adore you.
Your life brings gladness and rejoicing, blossoming and abundance.
In your life we find our joy: we would live to your glory.
God, keep us in your holy way: **That we may sing your praise.**

O God of freedom, we adore you.
Your presence strengthens, encourages and saves.
In your presence we are recognized and valued:
we would live to your glory.
God, keep us in your holy way: **That we may sing your praise.**

O God of hope, we adore you.
You are bringing all creation to healing and fulfilment.
Your Spirit refreshes the arid places of our world,
and makes the deserts into fruitful gardens.
God, keep us in your holy way: **That we may sing your praise.**

(16) Prayer of Confession

Loving Father, we are ashamed.
We know that you have heard us moaning and grumbling about other people. We confess that we have been cruel and unfeeling.
Father forgive us: **Renew your loving spirit within us.**

Loving Father, we are ashamed.
We have been impatient with others, not letting them fulfil tasks in their own time by their own ability. We have undermined their self-assurance and been arrogant in our own achievements.
Father, forgive us: **Renew your loving spirit within us.**

Loving Father, we are ashamed.
We have not encouraged others as we should. We have ignored their efforts and not given praise where it was due. We have been jealous of other peoples' achievements instead of rejoicing with them.
Father, forgive us: **Renew your loving spirit within us.**

Loving Father, may we carry the life of Christ
in affirming words and kindly deeds;
sharing your confidence and trust in us,
and helping each other to travel in hope
towards the coming of your kingdom.

(17) Prayer of Thanksgiving

Read James 5.7–10.
Lord, for the patience which comes from gratitude,
receiving the seed of your word in our hearts,
and the watering of your Spirit as it grows:
We give you thanks and praise.

For the strength which comes through waiting,
discerning your gentle presence in our midst
and recognizing your Spirit at work
in humble ways among us:
We give you thanks and praise.

For the peace which grows from compassion,
as we bear with each others' frailties
and endure the harassment of the world:
We give you thanks and praise.

(18) Prayer of Dedication

Lord, may we learn to see your kindness
in breaking bread with the hungry, in preaching the good news,
in bringing joy to the poor, and in setting prisoners free.
Lord, let us see with your eyes.

Lord, may we seek your Kingdom
in lifting up those who are burdened,
in offering a refuge for the stranger,
in standing with those who are powerless
and in pleading for the condemned.
Lord, let us love with your heart.

Lord, may we honour your glory
in giving sight to the blind, in making the deaf to hear,
in healing the diseased, and in raising the dead.
Lord, let us work with your hands.

(19) Meditation

Expected Lord – We do not wear camel-hair coats. We do not eat wild honey and locusts. We do not preach in the wilderness. But as John the Baptist prepared the way for you, so we make our preparations.

We do not have his charisma. We do not have strong words. We do not argue people into repentance. But as he prepared other people, so we too must help others to prepare themselves for your arrival. Preparation at this time usually means parcels and presents, but preparation for you, Lord, needs to be in prayer and praise.

Preparation at this time usually means food and festivities, but preparation for you, Lord, requires forgiveness.

Preparation at this time usually means crackers and cake, but preparation for you Lord, demands that we listen to you, so that we may know you when you come to us in Spirit and in fire.

(20) Prayer of Dismissal

Go into the world to tell others what you have heard and seen in Jesus.
Go into the world to share his healing, liberating love.

FOURTH SUNDAY OF ADVENT

Isaiah 7.10–16; Psalm 80.1–7, 17–19; Romans 1.1–7;
Matthew 1.18–25

CONCENTRATED COMPASSION

Presentation

Illustration: concentrated washing powder, high-powered batteries, lenses. Adverts convince us that concentrated products have more power in the same (or less) volume. All that is unnecessary has been removed, and the power is focussed in a smaller space. Discuss how sunlight, focussed through a magnifying glass, will burn paper, or the way in which lenses magnify the lamp of a light-house. Can these illustrations help us to understand how the love of God might be focussed or concentrated in Jesus? But God's power is only effective if it is received, accepted, offered, dedicated. This is the way of obedience, as walked by Joseph and Mary.

(21) Call to Worship

Isaiah 7.14; *or the following:*

Read Matthew 1.23.
God knows our human nature, our frailness and our vulnerability.
God was made human in Jesus.
Jesus knows our pain, he knows our joy.
God who became human is with us now.
Let us worship and praise the Lord our God.

(22) Prayer of Adoration

'Our God contracted to a span,
incomprehensibly made man.' (Charles Wesley)

What wonder is in these words, Lord!
That you, God of all creation – sun, moon, stars and planets – come to us as a vulnerable baby!
We stand in awe at the possibility of such an event.
We kneel in humility at such an act of giving.
It is beyond our understanding, Lord!

We have seen the adverts:
– a glass and a half of milk into one small chocolate bar
– double the amount of washes with a small box of powder
– the same size battery making the toy run twice as far.
Yet you did something far, far, greater –
arriving in our midst as a newborn child!
All that love so minutely concentrated.
Your love for all humanity as a single person.
You risked all on that astounding task;
you gave us everything you had to give.
We cannot find the words to express our wonder, our thanks, and our praise. How great you are, Lord; how great you are . . .

(23) Prayer of Confession and Thanksgiving

Forgive us, God of steadfast love, that so often we refuse to see you at work in ourselves, each other, and the world around us:
– for the sceptical attitudes which will not let us see your signs of hope
– for the prejudice which will not let us read your word of life
– for the obstacles which we place in the way of your healing power
– for the small-mindedness which restricts the flow of your grace.
Silence.
The Lord hears our prayer: **Thanks be to God.**

Thank you, God of steadfast love, that we can wait for your arrival in our midst:
– in gestures of caring and in words of encouragement
– in touches of gentleness and in smiles of relief
– in the lightening of burdens and in each tender embrace
– in shouts of laughter and in songs of joy.
Silence.
The Lord hears our prayer: **Thanks be to God.**

(24) Prayer of Dedication

Read Matthew 1.18–25.
Lord, you chose Mary.
You asked her to bear a child for you.
She was afraid, but she said yes. Yes – to your future.
She could not weigh all the consequences,
but she gave herself to your bidding.
Lord, make us strong to say ‘yes’ to your future for us.

Lord, you chose Joseph.
You met him in a dream and told him of your plans.
He was afraid, but he said yes. Yes – to your dream.
He did not know everything that would happen,
but he obeyed your word and accepted responsibility for your Son.
Lord, make us humble enough to obey you.

Lord, in choosing Mary and Joseph, you chose us.
You ask us to bear your grace, and to accept the task of caring.
You want us to carry the life of Jesus within us, and to make it our duty to love.
Lord, carry us beyond our fears.

Lord, your trust in us is overwhelming.
We are frightened by the responsibility – we cannot respond straight away. We ask questions: what will this mean? Where will I go? What will I do?
Lord, Mary and Joseph said 'yes' for us. Help us to join our 'yes' to theirs.

(25) Prayer of Petition or Dismissal

Living God, we call upon your love
as light to penetrate the unease, deceit and cruelty of the world.
In all places of shame: **Let your glory shine.**
In all homes of misery: **Let your glory shine.**
In all realms of hunger: **Let your glory shine.**
Wherever there is need or pain or suffering, let the concentrated compassion of your grace bring renewal and hope: **Let your glory shine!**

CHRISTMAS DAY

Isaiah 52.7–10; Psalm 98; Hebrews 1.1–4 (5–12); John 1.1–14

GOOD NEWS!

Presentation
Illustration: items associated with the celebration of good news: decorations, cards, invitation, flowers, cake, candles, songs etc. Discuss: how do we feel when we are carrying good news? What do we do to communicate it, share it, celebrate it? What are the similarities – or differences – between this and the way we celebrate Christmas? What is the 'good news' of Christmas that we want to communicate, celebrate and share?

(26) Call to Worship

Psalm 98.1–3 *or* 4–6; *or* Isaiah 9.2, 6–7.

(27) Prayer of Adoration and Thanksgiving

Gather items of good news or causes for celebration from among the congregation. These can be inserted into the prayer, or the prayer can stand as a summary of the list. A candle could be lit for every thanksgiving.

O God of all joy, we give you thanks and praise, for you have created the world, given us life, and provided for all our needs.
O sing to the Lord a new song: **For he has done marvellous things!**

For you have given us endurance in times of suffering, and courage in all our distress . . .
O sing to the Lord a new song: **For he has done marvellous things!**

For you have refreshed us when we grew weary, and given us peace in the midst of trouble . . .
O sing to the Lord a new song: **For he has done marvellous things!**

For you have brought us comfort when we were sorrowful, and consoled us in our grieving . . .
O sing to the Lord a new song: **For he has done marvellous things!**

For you have healed us when we were sick, revived us when we were discouraged, and renewed us when we were downhearted . . .
O sing to the Lord a new song: **For he has done marvellous things!**

For you have given us new life in Christ, that as he is born into the world, we can know new hope, new faith, new joy . . .
O sing to the Lord a new song: **For he has done marvellous things!**

(28) Prayer of Affirmation

Can be used after a silent or extempore confession or intercession.

Lord Jesus, you are the light there in the beginning, bringing all things into life, and giving knowledge and wisdom to all people.
You are our light: **And the darkness cannot overcome you.**

Lord Jesus, you are the light coming into the world, looking for those who will believe, who are ready to be changed into children of God.
You are our light: **And the darkness cannot overcome you.**

Lord Jesus, you are the light coming to us, and we receive you with open, trembling hands, wondering at your grace, marvelling at your glory.
You are our light: **And the darkness cannot overcome you.**

(29) Prayer of Petition or Dedication

God of all goodness and love,
as your Son Jesus Christ has appeared among us in grace,
offering himself into our life and death in the greatest mercy;
may we offer ourselves into the joys and sorrows of others,
as kindness, as healing, as hope.

God of all riches and majesty,
as your Son Jesus Christ received the gifts of strangers,
taking his place among those who knew their need of others;
may we learn the generosity of gratitude,
and so encourage the growth of talents for the blessing of all.

God of all wisdom and wonder,
as your Son Jesus Christ was heralded by visions and dreams,
revealed by signs in heaven and the songs of angels:
may we so radiate glad and tender zeal
that we may spread your joyous peace in word and deed.

(30) Prayer of Dedication or Dismissal

Go into the light, taking bread to feed the hungry, peace to heal those who are wounded, and hope to renew those bowed down by doubt or despair:
Living God, lead us from light into light.

Go into the light, taking encouragement to those in difficulty, compassion to comfort those who grieve, and joy to share with the lonely:
Living God, lead us from light into light.

Go into the light, as bringers of good news, as bearers of grace, as those who carry mercy, and as witnesses to God's glory:
Living God, lead us from light into light.

(31) Prayer of Dismissal

Let us go into the day to celebrate God-with-us.
Let us go together to share God's mercy with all people.
Let us go in peace to live in God's joy.

FIRST SUNDAY OF CHRISTMAS

Isaiah 63.7–9; Psalm 148; Hebrews 2.10–18; Matthew 2.13–23

GOOD NEWS?

Presentation

Illustration: shadows. Demonstrate with a torch or lamp the way that strong light creates shadows. Discuss: what is the 'shadow side' of Christmas? – the uncertainty over lodgings, the pain of birth, the dirt of the stable, the murder of innocent children. We celebrate God-with-us in both the light and the shade, though the shadows leave us with uncomfortable questions.

(32) Call to Worship

Psalm 148.1–2, 13 *or* Isaiah 63.7; *or the following:*

The promise has been kept.
A new hope is given.
The Son of God is born.
We are here to greet him with wonder and with joy.
Let us praise and worship the living God revealed in human form.

(33) Prayer of Adoration

O God of creation, for you and through you all things exist. You love us and know our needs: **We adore you.**

O God of all people, you have revealed yourself to us as Father and friend. You love us and know our needs: **We adore you.**

O God of grace, yours is an abundant and bountiful grace, ever flowing for our nourishment, nurture and care. You love us and know our needs: **We adore you.**

O God of tomorrow, in your saving presence we find our freedom; in your tenderness we find our strength; in your promise we place our trust, now and forever.

(34) Meditation

The four readers start out as newspaper sellers, standing apart, who then begin to reflect together on the news they are advertising.

Voice 1: Read all about it! Mystery. Suspense. Murder!
Voice 2: Read all about it! The Son of God, born in a stable!
Voice 3: Read all about it! Narrow escape from massacre!
Voice 4: Read all about it! Herod murders the children!
Voice 1: Read all about it! It's a gripping story!
Voice 2: What a mystery – where did the baby Jesus come from?
Voice 3: What suspense – where can she have the baby? Will they get away? Where can they go?
Voice 4: Put like that it hardly sounds true – like something out of a novel, or Hollywood, or a thriller on TV.
Voice 1: Or just an everyday news story!
Voice 2: But it happened! The mighty God – all that mystery – made known to us in a baby!
Voice 3: The secret God, who keeps us waiting – is now born! The living God of new life escapes from death.
Voice 4: But the others didn't. The innocents never do.
Voice 1: Yes, we know. But just listen to the wonder of it! We read about it in the Gospels, we celebrate it every December, we say it in the Creed . . .
Voice 2: It's not a fairytale.
Voice 3: It happened.
Voice 4: So you say.
Voice 1: I know it sounds fantastic, unbelievable, out of this world. But we know it's true! It happened for us!
Voice 2: Marvel at the miracle of it.
Voice 3: What a blessing! Can't we just kneel in awe and wonder?
Voice 4: You mean like the people in the stable. In all that muck?
Voice 1: For him? Yes! For Jesus Christ. (*kneels*)
Voice 2: For the Saviour of the World. The Mighty God. (*kneels*)
Voice 3: Wonderful Counsellor. Everlasting Father. (*kneels*)
Voice 4: Not for them – but for the Prince of Peace. (*kneels*)

(35) Prayer of Confession and Acknowledgment

Hold us, God of hope, as we confess to you the sin and shame in our lives, and the sin and shame of the world of which we are part.
Silence.

Encourage us, God of mercy, as we ask your blessing on those relationships which we know fall short of your high love.
Silence.

Guide us, God of wisdom, as we seek to know the right, and the courage to establish your holiness in our homes and our communities.
Silence.

(36) Prayer of Thanksgiving

Caring God, as you have created all children for joy, we give you thanks for the children in our midst, and the children we carry in our hearts.
Merciful Jesus, as you blessed marriage and family life, we give you thanks for our relationships of love and friendship.
Living Spirit, as you lead us through sorrow to praise, we give you thanks for that grace which grants peace even in the midst of suffering, and which transforms our fear into trust and hope.

(37) Prayer of Petition

For those who run from threat or fighting, hunger or abuse:
Lord, be a sheltering hand.
For those who cannot run, who are in danger themselves and those they love:
Lord, be a guarding hand.
For those who, are not protected, and who are broken in body, mind, heart or soul:
Lord be a healing hand.
Where we can offer help to those in need or want or fear:
Lord be a strengthening hand.
That right may prevail, the weak be protected and the wicked brought to account:
Lord be a mighty hand.

(38) Prayer of Dismissal

Jesus has come into the world to give us faith.
We will carry the faith with us.
Jesus has come into the world to give us hope.
We will carry the hope with us.
Jesus has come into the world to give us love.
We will carry the love with us.
Jesus has come into the world to give us joy and praising, singing and dancing:
That all may know that Jesus has come into the world.

SECOND SUNDAY OF CHRISTMAS

(if before 6 January)

Jeremiah 31.7–14 (alternative reading Ecclesiasticus 24.1–12);
Psalm 147.12–20 (alternative canticle Wisdom of Solomon 10.15–21);
Ephesians 1.3–14; John 1.(1–9) 10–18

THE PROMISE IS FULFILLED!

Presentation
Illustration: a flourishing garden. Demonstrate and discuss the difference between a bucket of sand and a well-tended pot plant. Draw out the importance of environment, cultivation, care and commitment in the creation of a beautiful garden. Christ is God's nurturing and nourishing care for us, not only urging us to change, but making that transformation possible – if we co-operate.

(40) Call to Worship

Psalm 147.1, 12–13 *or* Jeremiah 31.7, 10.

(41) Prayer of Adoration

We praise you, Lord, we proclaim your grace,
for you have saved us, your people, and gathered us here;
caring for the weak and the frail,
and turning our griefs into joys:
We praise you, Lord God, we adore you.

We praise you, Lord, we proclaim your grace,
for you have fulfilled your promise to us, your people;
consoling those who weep, befriending the lonely,
refreshing those who thirst in spirit,
and leading the wanderers home:
We praise you, Lord God, we adore you.

We praise you, Lord, we proclaim your grace,
for your radiance has illumined our night,
and you have brought us from poverty to abundance;
a time of giving and feasting, riches and laughter,
light and gladness, joy and dancing:
We praise you, Lord God, we adore you.

(42) Prayer of Confession

O Christ the Light, you come to us as Word, as Wisdom,
as God's creative life yearning to do a new thing in the world.
But we like our own ideas and ways; we prefer to remain pure;
we remain within our circle because we want to know who is on our side.
Silence.

O Christ the Light, you come to us as Truth, as Glory.
You tell us our story, but in a way we have not heard before.
You show us that our tradition was larger than we had imagined.
You understand our experience, but you lead us beyond it.
And it frightens us. We do not want to recognize ourselves like this.
So we turn aside from knowing; we do not want you close;
we refuse to place in you our trust;
we drown out your song with a clamour of our own.
Silence.

O Christ the Light, you come to us as the power to change,
the strengthening grace to be different,
to live an alternative future, and to transform the world.
May we grow into wiser versions of ourselves,
seeking your fullness, your maturity, your freedom,
that wisdom and grace may be made flesh in us,
and we may witness to your glory.

(43) Prayer of Thanksgiving

Thanks be to God,
for bread and word to feed body and mind;
love and prayer to nourish heart and soul;
and for the cleansing of the Spirit meeting our spirit:
Thanks be to God.

Thanks be to God,
for the lavishness of provision,
for the promise fulfilled,
and for the wonder of our inheritance in Christ:
Thanks be to God.

Thanks be to God,
who has chosen us in love,
trained us in compassion,
and who sustains us in faith and hope:
Thanks be to God.

(44) Prayer of Petition

Living God, your love flows throughout creation,
boundless and free, without limit or constraint,
except where you are resisted and refused:
Immerse us in the flow of your healing waters.

You would fold all in the grace of your compassionate purpose,
lavishing upon us the riches of companionship,
the mercy of forgiveness, the joyous pain of service:
Carry us on your river of peace.

You have given us insights into the unplumbed depths of your mystery. We bear a knowledge of your wisdom and your intent, that desire which would bring all into your liberation and your joy:
Draw us beyond the shore of your promise known into the sea of adoring praise.

(45) Prayer of Dedication

O God of the transforming Spring,
well up within our hearts
as life, as love, as peace, as joy;
that new hopes may be sown in the world.
May others' hearts find refreshment through us,
and through our weeding, digging, planting
in the soil of our daily lives,
may gardens grow in ruined towns and desert places.

(46) Prayer of Dismissal

Let us receive the blessing of God, for the promise is fulfilled and our hope is come. Let us live in rejoicing, for the promise is fulfilled, and God's joy is ours. Let us offer the grace of God, for the promise is fulfilled, and all are invited to the feast of life.